'Thom's writing is both vivid and compelling . . . attuned to the timeless antagonisms of intimacy'
DAISY LAFARGE

'A spry tale of friendship and desire. *Summer Hours* is astute, funny and fizzing with life'
MALACHY TALLACK

'Everything about this book is alive. I inhaled it'
MARIA SLEDMERE

'I love Alessandra Thom's writing. *Summer Hours* is witty, immersive . . . and beautifully written'
RODGE GLASS

SUMMER HOURS

SUMMER HOURS

ALESSANDRA THOM

Polygon

First published in hardback in Great Britain in 2025
by Polygon, an imprint of Birlinn Ltd

Birlinn Ltd | West Newington House
10 Newington Road | Edinburgh | EH9 1QS

9 8 7 6 5 4 3 2 1

www.polygonbooks.co.uk

Copyright © Alessandra Thom, 2025

The right of Alessandra Thom to be identified as the author of this work has been asserted in accordance with the Copyright, Designs and Patents Act 1988.

All rights reserved. No part of this publication may be reproduced, stored, or transmitted in any form, or by any means electronic, mechanical or photocopying, recording or otherwise, without the express written permission of the publisher.

ISBN 978 1 84697 671 1
EBOOK ISBN 978 1 78885 664 5

British Library Cataloguing-in-Publication Data
A catalogue record for this book is available on request from the British Library.

The publisher acknowledges support from the National Lottery through Creative Scotland towards the publication of this title.

Typeset in Bembo Book MT Pro by The Foundry, Edinburgh
Printed and bound in Great Britain by Clays Ltd, Elcograf S.p.A.

For Rachel

ONE: APRIL 2018

TONIGHT, EVE TELLS ROISIN, they are going to the reservoir. It has been planned for weeks, apparently. It is a humid, uncharacteristically hot day in April – there are rumours of a summer heatwave – and Edinburgh has a soft orange tint to it. The air reeks of hops, but nobody cares because the whole city is out drinking cans in a park with warm sunburn lines down their shoulders where their bra straps betrayed them.

Roisin and Eve are sitting in Roisin's flat, each in a corner of the empty bath. They have propped open the window with a short plank of wood. The sun is pouring in, they're picking at a bag of strawberry laces, and they've been drinking berry-flavoured wine all afternoon in fuzzy room-temperature sips. Eve bought it from Oddbins instead of from the supermarket, but Roisin thinks it just tastes like Echo Falls. She thinks that any wine tastes like Echo Falls when it's drunk from a mug in a bath. She does not tell Eve this.

Eve thinks that it's best practice to be tipsy in warm weather, so that you remember the summer in a haze rather than a stark white light. Like putting an Instagram filter on your own memories. Roisin leans her head back against the cool tiles and watches the sun ripple on the white walls.

'You must have forgotten, I definitely told you.'

'Yeah, I think you probably did,' Roisin lies. 'Which reservoir?'

'Is there more than one?'

Roisin hesitates, not sure if Eve doesn't know that there is more than one, or if she means there's only one good one so why would you go anywhere else?

'Yeah, there's more than one,' Roisin says, deciding on the former.

'Right yeah, of course.' Eve motions at her for more wine. Roisin leans over the side of the bath and tops up her mug with the contents of the sticky bottle, licking the top afterward to stop it dripping.

'Anyway,' Eve says. 'Claire said she'd drive us, so we don't need to know which one.'

She takes a sip and sticks her head out of the window, eyes closed against the sun.

Claire is Eve's boyfriend's twin sister, a self-defined free spirit. She has a husband who she calls her *partner*. Roisin has never met him, and she sometimes wonders if Claire has made him up. Roisin does not like being

APRIL

around Claire. She makes her feel very young, and very small.

'Isn't Claire great? She gave me this last week.'

Eve sticks her pasty leg out and pulls up her long skirt to display a silver anklet. Roisin tells her it's gorgeous, and Eve twists her foot backwards and forwards, admiring herself.

Roisin's flatmate Calum slouches through, chaps softly on the door and tries very hard not to make eye contact with either of them. He asks the floor if it'd like a cup of tea, and Roisin tells him that would be nice. Eve waggles her wine at him in response. He slouches off.

'He's a wee freak,' Eve says. She leans even further out of the window. He is, but mostly he just doesn't like Eve.

Cal has a proper job. He gets up at eight every day, packs a lunch and a flask of tea, and then he puts on a little backpack and goes and sits behind a computer until five. This is why he has the big room and Roisin has the boxroom with the bed on a platform which she has to climb a ladder to get to.

Roisin used to work in a café on Leith Walk. The whole place was a symptom of gentrification with its monstera plants and its cold brew and its vegan raw cakes that nobody who lives in proximity to Leith Walk could possibly want. She got sacked last week after sleeping through a shift. It was her third no-show in a fortnight. When you are traipsing over North Bridge at four o'clock in the morning with a friend like Eve, matters like work and paying rent seem pretty trivial. Roisin applied for an overdraft last week, but RBS declined her. This was a revelation: that you can be so shit with money that a bank won't allow you to get into debt.

Eve does not have a job either. She arrived without warning one windy Saturday because her parents had been pissing her off. She asked if she could sleep on the sofa for a week, and Roisin of course said yes, but the week-mark passed without comment, and Eve has not mentioned leaving since. She has only been crashing for a couple of months, but in that time she has managed to mark the flat indelibly with her presence.

She does not pay rent, but she keeps buying things. She has a hundred different throws and cushions, and the floor of the living room is littered with Lush makeup and weird hair potions from the herbal skincare shop across from Leith Walk Oddbins. She keeps collecting prints of Portobello from cafés in Abbeyhill, and she has pinned them to the walls. She has bought a tall rhododendron with huge blowsy red flowers. You are not supposed to keep them as houseplants; it is wilting softly into its mud. She has placed it proudly into a very heavy terracotta pot.

APRIL

The sofa where she sleeps is not quite as comfortably fluffy as it used to be. Eve has indented it permanently with her form. For a while she took the sheets and the duvet off the sofa and tucked them up into a neat pile in the corner every morning after she woke up. She stopped doing this a while ago. Roisin can't remember when.

Roisin kicks Eve's legs off of her, clambers out of the bath and stumbles through to the kitchen. The wine has affected her more than she thought it had, and the room seems to tilt gently.

Something floral is wafting its way towards her. Cal has made himself a wee 'tea station' on the kitchen windowsill so he can spy on their neighbours while he makes a cuppa. There is a girl across the street who they are both in love with. She hangs out of her window every morning with a cigarette and a tiny wee espresso cup, and she dances, flailing her arms about to a beat neither of them can hear. A sheet of A4 printer paper is taped to her window – it reads FUCK in scrawling sharpie. Eve thinks she is attention-seeking.

Cal is making himself Earl Grey tea in the nice teapot, with the nice tea leaves. Eve bought them. Roisin doesn't think she knows he's been nicking them.

'We're going to the reservoir tonight if you want to come?' Roisin asks him. She really wants him to come, but she doesn't want him to know that.

'Who's we?'

'Eve, her boyfriend and Claire.'

She leans against the sink and watches him try to avoid eye contact with her. His brow is tightly furrowed, and he's squashing the leaves hard against the side of the strainer with a teaspoon.

'D'you want to come then?'

'Mm, a would, but am shattered, thanks though.'

She squints at him. The sun has painted him a golden-brown aura, which Roisin finds interesting because he always read to her as a golden-brown kind of person. She promised Cal that this afternoon she would speak to Eve about her moving out, but she hasn't.

Eve is fun! Fucking about with her is like being a teenager again, and Roisin doesn't want it to end. Since Eve arrived and started paying for her drink, Roisin's days off have turned into a never-ending conveyor belt of wine in the park, beer on Portobello beach, gin and tonics in hot, sweaty, blue-tinted clubs with underagers dancing like their lives depend on it, all surrounded by Eve's very best friends who she met yesterday or a week ago or just this very second darling! She's made more friends here in two months than Roisin has in years. And now they're Roisin's friends too because she is friends with Eve, and when they recognise her they go, Oh! You're Eve's pal right? And it's like she has entry into a secret club and the password is Eve12345!

Roisin thinks instead that if he wants to ask her to leave then he should do it himself. It's not her responsibility just because she's her friend. He leaves with his cup of tea, and she leans against the kitchen sink, letting her head spin pleasantly. The girl across the road is leaning out of the window smoking in a sombre, French-film kind of way.

Eve calls through a fifteen-minute warning: Claire has just texted her, she's on her way. Roisin isn't sure if she can face this. She thinks she'd like to stand at this window and watch the girl blow smoke rings all evening instead.

She takes one of Cal's locally brewed IPAs from the fridge (green sharpie marking his territory in a half-moon C) and goes back through to the bathroom. She clambers into the bath and starts to drink it in long gulps.

'Slow down, Roisin, wow.'

Eve looks at her, head tilted analytically. 'Claire's gone sober,' she tells her. 'She's gone on this diet. You know, maybe you should try it too. It's so important to treat your body well, you know, not load it up with chemicals and crap.'

She peels a strawberry lace out of the packet and into her mouth.

Her eyes light up when she talks about Claire.

Roisin often thinks that she could talk about her all day long without pause for breath.

She often catches her staring at Claire's hands. They're tanned and lean with very short nails, and she has lots of artfully mismatched stick-and-poke hand tattoos she got from friends and acquaintances in far-flung cities, and if you ask her about them she'll go into excruciating detail about exactly when and where and from whom she got them. She does have very nice hands, but nobody looks at them like Eve does. Eve looks at them like she's imagining what they would feel like inside her.

Roisin can't see the smoking girl from the bathroom window. Eve might be able to, but Roisin is sitting in the wrong side of the bath. The sun has moved slightly so now Eve gets it all, while Roisin is sitting in partial shade. And her back is pressed uncomfortably against the taps. Eve tilts her head back and closes her eyes, drinking the light in.

★

The car window is open, and the cool air buffets against Roisin's skin, whipping her hair back gently. She can see rolling hills, tiny wee burns running through the valleys of soft moss, sparrows and swallows and thumb-sized blue tits chasing after each other.

APRIL

'A man drowned here last summer.'

Eve is stretching in the passenger seat. She keeps taking her short blonde hair in and out of a ponytail, as if unable to get it to look exactly how she wants it to, incapable of accepting anything less than perfect appearance.

Her boyfriend turns briefly to grin at Claire and Roisin in the back, and interrupts his girlfriend to ask them how they're doing back there. Claire and Roisin both nod and grunt. He demanded to drive the second they arrived at his place because Claire doesn't know the roads like he does.

Their accents are very different for two people brought up together. Eve told Roisin they were raised here by English parents. Traces of Edinburgh still linger in the corners of their mouths, but Claire has refined hers so that you would suspect southeast England rather than southeast Scotland. He, on the other hand, has developed a strange Americanised lilt in his intonation, normally only found in men who are chronically online.

Roisin noticed Eve's accent smooth out at the edges the second Claire picked them up. With a twinge of self-loathing, she noticed her own do the same.

Eve is telling the car all about how Roisin has lost her job. Roisin wishes she wouldn't, but honestly there is no way to stop Eve once she gets going. She is pitching it as though it is a worker's rights story, rather than a lazy, hungover twentysomething's story.

To Eve it is fun and interesting to have slept through your shift and said fuck you to capitalism, but to Roisin it is a reminder of how unqualified she is for any job. She has no money to pay Eve back. Not for anything, not even the wine and the strawberry laces. Eve might be sponging off her for her sofa, but there is no number attached to that, no clear value. Their friendship has become like a set of old kitchen scales to which they each add and subtract every good deed and every drink bought. The precarious equilibrium of their relationship depends upon them each feeling in debt to the other. Each of them has always pushed at the boundaries of acceptable behaviour, seeing how much they could get out of the other. A week on the sofa becomes a month. *Could you spot me this drink?* turns into *Can you pay for the entire night and the taxi home?*

Roisin stares out of the window and tries to tune Eve out. They're not far from the reservoir now; the shape of the road is becoming familiar, and Roisin thinks she recognises the landscape of the sloping hills beyond. She came here once with Cal when they were in university and is surprised to find she can still remember the drive.

Eve's boyfriend parks wonkily on a grass verge, and they all tumble out of the car. It's still a beautiful day,

APRIL

turning slowly into a rare evening in late spring when the sky finally begins to shake off the dark like a winter coat and the days feel like they last a lifetime and there's that pinky gold glow about everyone's skin. Claire fashions a step stool out of two rocks and a plank of wood and covers the barbed-wire fence with a large strip of cardboard from the boot of the car.

'You first.'

Roisin balances one foot obediently on the makeshift step and tries to vault over to the other side, but the cardboard slips right at the last second, and she catches the inside of her leg on a barb, landing hard on her back.

She lies stunned for a moment, a pain twinging near her ankle, dulled by the alcohol. She feels too big for her own body. She raises her neck up, breathless, to look over, but her vision is blurry and twisted, and the trees shift about as though they are people jostling in a crowd, talking urgently to one another, trying to get their points across.

Nobody notices. Claire walks back over to the car where they're unloading and chatting. Roisin wipes the trickle of blood off her leg with her sleeve. It slowly stains the pale blue fabric a deep, dark red. Her head pounds, and she has the sensation of having too much empty space between her ears. She moves very slowly into a seated position and tries to breathe deeply.

As she sits there, winded, Eve's boyfriend saunters over and dumps the firewood and a rucksack full of alcohol over the fence at her feet and turns back around to head to the car. He does not seem to find it unusual that she is on the ground.

Roisin thinks he's a dick. He brews his own kombucha. Roisin knows this because he told her as they were loading his shit into Claire's car. He stood with one skinny leg up on the edge of the car boot facing straight towards her, shifting his weight between each foot so that he was almost doing lunges.

Roisin gets to her feet and heads cautiously down through the woods to the edge of the water.

The reservoir is beautiful. The water laps gently against the weedy rocks with barely a sound. The hills behind frame the loch like a postcard, and there is a wee island in the middle, just too far away to swim to.

Nobody is supposed to swim in the reservoirs at all because of the dams, which occasionally will pull underwater currents towards the grates as if they were giant plugholes, but the second it gets above 15 degrees everyone in Scotland loses their head and behaves as if they live in a theme park. It's not really the currents that cause the most deaths anyway. The reservoirs look deeper than they are; most people die from overestimating their depths and diving into the shallows from rowing boats.

APRIL

Wee ones splash each other in the shallows and three different groups of paddleboarders all move serenely, seemingly without effort, across the horizon. There are more barbecues than Roisin can count.

On the hillside in the horizon someone has carved out a word by manipulating bushes to grow in the shape of letters. It looks like LEVE, but it could well be LOVE or LIVE.

Roisin watches as Claire walks over to a group of strangers surrounded by tents pitched where the trees meet the sand and greets them enthusiastically. This is a surprise. Roisin didn't realise they were coming here to meet more people.

There are around fifteen of them, all crouching around an attempt at a fire – a small stack of newspaper, twigs, and some green branches which they have clearly just snapped off a nearby tree. It's smoking heavily.

Roisin wonders how long they have been here. The tents sag heavily with rainfall and rotting leaves. Most of them have the wide-eyed look of someone who has not yet come down from last night's trip.

They stand up ceremoniously when Claire and Roisin come over, and each one introduces themselves with a weighted deliberation, like a bad spoken-word performance. Their accents are softly neutral. English, or maybe American. Nobody has a real name

– Razz, Bear, Often, Oak – but all of them stumble over Roisin's.

As she stands and tries to engage in the chat – mostly anecdotes about people Roisin has never heard of – she notices a very young, eerily thin wee boy toddling around the group, putting soft brown leaves and sand into his mouth, and she wonders what the fuck she is doing here.

Roisin decides to build a real fire. The key is to get a good base layer and to find really big rocks to go around the edge so that when the logs crumble into bright amber toffee through a kind of mystic alchemy they can keep burning at the bottom and the wind won't blow them out.

Eve is laughing with Claire and a small group of their friends: people with deep, even tans. Eve sticks out here too, a bit – her hair is too obviously box-dyed, her makeup just too thick. Her boyfriend is already swimming, cutting a V-shaped line of rippled water straight out into the reservoir.

Roisin lights a match and touches it gently to the twisted-up newspaper she's tangled around the logs. She watches as the face of a footballer's wife is eaten up by the flame.

The sun is low, resting just above the horizon. Roisin decides to stop feeling out of place. These people are not her people, but then who are her people? She's done yoga. She has been known to buy organic veg from Easter Greens when she wants people to notice her walking home holding brown paper bags filled with kale and avocado.

She blows a thin line of air into the bottom of the fire and watches it begin to lick at the wood. In her peripheral vision she can see Eve moving over to her. Eve proffers an enamel cup and fills it up to the brim with fizzy white wine.

'Thank fuck,' Roisin says.

'What?'

'Thank fuck this is alcoholic.'

Eve laughs. Then she says, almost apologetically, 'I didn't know there would be all these people here. He didn't tell me.' She gestures back at her boyfriend, now doing a clean backstroke across the loch.

Roisin shrugs. 'It's fine. Don't worry about it.'

They sit and drink and look at the fire. Eve and Roisin have known each other for a very long time. They did their first communion together at the cathedral. There is a photo Roisin keeps of the two of them in the back pocket of an old journal. They are both stood in starched white, smiling slightly to the left of the camera, where out of shot two of the boys were trading Pokémon cards. Roisin and Eve both wore kitten heels and bright white dresses and polyester veils and they walked down the aisle slowly, slowly.

Roisin remembers ripping off her dress in a fiery act of rebellion, tearing around the room in her tights and vest hoping someone would pay her attention, but Eve sat and waited at the table with her hands crossed on her lap for the adults to finish.

They are both chameleons, she and Eve, but for Eve it comes a bit more naturally, which is where they differ. Eve seems to instinctively know what people want from her.

'I might go for a swim,' Eve says.

Roisin nods in response.

'Yeah.' Eve nods too, as though to reassure herself this is the right decision. 'I think Claire's going in.'

Roisin pokes at the fire with a stick. It's burning properly now, and there's a thick heat coming off it.

Eve's boyfriend crunches his way up the pebbled shore to the fire and stands dripping onto them for a moment before wrapping himself up in a towel like a little boy. It's orange and faded. The colour reminds Roisin of a bowl of cornflakes.

He envelopes Eve in a huge bear hug, and she squeals as he shakes droplets of frozen water all over her. Three large drops plop into Roisin's drink.

He pushes Eve gently off the driftwood then swings his dripping legs over the log and sits behind her with one leg on either side, pulling her back into his crotch and wrapping his arms around her. He strokes Eve's hair repeatedly behind her ear, like she's a spaniel. Eve ducks out of his reach and pours herself more wine.

He starts to peel off his neoprene swimming socks with an intense focus. They are too small for him, and now that they're wet, he's struggling to get them off. Eve watches him from behind her mug with vague disgust.

For a long time now Eve has had a tendency to go for men she dislikes. Men so unremarkable that now Roisin struggles to recall their faces. Roisin assumes it gives Eve a sort of power in the relationship, knowing that she doesn't care enough about them for them to be able to hurt her. They can say what they want to her, do what they want to her, but she doesn't respect them enough for it to make any difference. She feels like she has the upper hand. It makes Roisin wonder whether Eve likes her.

Roisin's phone buzzes in her pocket. She has a text from her old boss Miriam telling her that if she comes in now she can have her old job back. Someone else has decided to not show up for their shift. Every now and then Miriam gets really enthusiastic about some local band and the place stays open late for a *chilled-out evening of vibey music* serving teensy little posh canapés and free wine. It's time-and-a-half pay so Roisin always volunteers for the shifts, plus she gets to take home the leftovers. Cal's a fan of the smoked-salmon blinis.

If Roisin can get someone to come and pick her up then she can leave. Maybe it would be more fun to sit behind a café bar for four hours than watch Eve's boyfriend attempt to fondle her. Roisin stands up and begins to pull on her jumper.

'Yeah so this guy I knew died here,' Eve is saying. 'He was out here with some friends –'

'Who is it?' Her boyfriend interrupts her, looking at Roisin.

'It's my boss. I can have my job back if I go in now.'

'Ah shit.' Eve sits up. 'I'm sure Claire can drive you there? I don't know where she is though.'

Roisin is taken aback by Eve's willingness to help. Either she was trying to impress them in the car and isn't really naïve enough to think that a job is pointless, or she wants Roisin gone. Either way it gives Roisin even more reason to leave.

All three of them start scanning the horizon. There's nobody by the tents anymore: everyone seems to be sitting by the shore or in the water.

'I think she's swimming,' Eve's boyfriend says.

He points to a small speck far from the shoreline, a head bobbing in and out of the water rhythmically.

'I'll swim out,' he says, standing up and stretching his arms above his head. He kisses Eve on the top of her head and jogs to the shoreline. He is wearing red shorts that are horribly reminiscent of *Baywatch*.

APRIL

In the distance, Eve's boyfriend has reached his sister. He waves his arms around, trying to tread water and explain himself at the same time.

Claire flips onto her back and starts to float, starfished. He swims back to shore.

'Sorry ladies, she's been drinking! So have I, or I'd drive you.'

So much for Claire going sober.

'It's fine,' Roisin says. 'Whatever.'

Eve has clearly already lost interest in the conversation; she is watching Claire swim with an intense focus.

Roisin takes out her phone and looks up how much a taxi would cost from here, and then she puts her phone away again because she doesn't have £60 to spend on a cab fare to go to a workplace that has already let her go in order to escape people who are supposed to be her friends.

And if she's honest with herself, she can't help but be a little relieved that Claire can't take her. It's hard having a job and also trying to be young and carefree. She doesn't really want to work at all.

Roisin turns her phone off. The sun moves behind a cloud. It's a relief. Roisin didn't realise how scrunched up her face had been against the light, but relaxing it now almost hurts. The reservoir turns a deep dark blue-black, and the fire stands out against the rest of the shore. She doesn't think she built the wall around it well enough; a couple of rocks have tumbled into the centre. Not enough for it to blow out, and by this point the fire is roaring, but she wants to pull her sleeve over her hand and pick them up, put them back in their place so that the row is even again.

Her stomach is sore. The wine they drank earlier is sitting in the bottom of it like stagnant water, and she wonders when they will be eating. She and Eve went out for lunch, but the menu was so pricey Roisin said she wasn't hungry and got a coffee instead. She had sort of hoped Eve would pay for her, but she didn't.

Eve is fiddling with the anklet Claire gave her. It glints red in the glow from the fire.

'I'm going to go swimming,' Eve says. 'Claire will be waiting for me: I told her I'd come and join her.'

Roisin stands up and shimmies out of her shorts. 'I'm coming too.'

The sun is beginning to set, and the sky is turning gold at the edges; the loch looks like a postcard slowly being eaten up by flames.

The water is sharply cold, the sunset like an oil slick on the shallows.

The sandy loch bed slips slightly under Roisin's feet. She treads carefully in the shallows, while Eve wades out in front of her. Seeing Eve in the water makes Roisin nervous: neither she nor Eve are strong

APRIL

swimmers. Claire is right in the middle of the reservoir, a little pin bobbing in the distance. Roisin watches as Eve reaches the end of the shallow shelf then hesitates.

Roisin takes a deep breath in and tries not to squeal as she wades deeper into the loch, splashing her chest rhythmically with the water in a futile attempt to make the experience less awful, reaching Eve when she is waist-deep.

The water is so still it's like a mirror. Both their faces are reflected, rippling across the surface of the water. They stand together for a while, watching Claire as she propels herself on her back over the top of the water.

The light is bouncing off Eve's shoulders – you can see every freckle on her back – and her hair is turned to gold by the setting sun. Roisin studies her reflection in the rippling loch as Eve smiles softly at her, her lips slightly parted, and Roisin has to stop herself from reaching out and brushing them with her thumb.

Instead she pulls herself up then down hard, plunging her head and shoulders under; the baptism is so cold she has to force herself not to gasp. She holds her breath, pulls herself forward and lets herself float there for a second, suspended. The shrieks of children playing and adults laughing are muffled here, ears under the cool green. Fronds of a slippery plant lick at Roisin's upper arms, or maybe it's her hair, or maybe it's Eve, blowing her cool breath over her neck.

She pulls her arms out in front of her and pushes herself out, coming up for air with a splutter.

Claire has swum over to them and now sculls casually, watching Roisin cough. Her dark hair has been slicked back by the water.

The cold shock of the loch seems to have untangled the knot in Roisin's stomach.

Eve looks at them both expectantly. Then she bursts out: 'A man drowned here last summer. He was in one of those wee canoes with his friends, my friends, actually, I know them from way back, anyway I think they'd been drinking or something and they were taking turns to jump off the boat into the water and he dived instead of just jumping in. The water's so shallow here, you know, because it's man-made, that he broke his wrists and cracked his head off the bottom of the loch and died. Like that.' She tries to click her fingers, but they're wet, and it doesn't work.

'So he didn't really drown, then,' Claire says. 'He died of a head injury.'

Eve shrugs and swills the water around with her hands, creating a little whirlpool that separates her from the other two women. Roisin follows Eve's gaze, fixed on Claire striding away through the shallows, squeezing the water from her hair.

The light is beginning to fade and turn cold. A breeze has picked up, skimming over the gentle waves. Roisin's arms are heavy from the damp chill of the loch, and her head feels weighed down by her frozen, sopping hair. Eve falls backwards gently, lying on her back in the water. She has her eyes closed. Her blonde hair, tinted a strange amber by the water, spirals out from her head in a milky cloud, and Roisin is reminded of Ophelia, surrounded by sweet flowers in the soft water.

Eve is being cradled by slippery dark fingers of loch weeds which gouge into her waist as she floats deeper out into the water.

Claire is watching Roisin watch Eve.

Roisin smiles and raises her hand to her awkwardly. Claire doesn't respond, just shifts her gaze so that she is looking over to the hills again.

They look like a patchwork quilt, alternating woods and sheep. The misshapen bushes are even further distorted in the fading light so that Roisin can't make out any of the letters; instead they form what looks like a crude drawing of a dark, spiky fire. She squints at it. The last time she came to the reservoir Cal set his t-shirt on fire.

Back then they had a friend whose name Roisin can't remember now, who always asked for hot milk instead of tea and who had a car, so the three of them would leave the city on nice days to explore the surrounding area. In the winter they would drive to

Portobello and eat fish, chips and mushy peas huddled by the boardwalk in the biting cold wind.

In the summers, or on those rare days when the weather was warm, Portobello became like the Meadows – so packed full of people that going for a walk became an obstacle course – so they would head for places they thought would be less busy. The reservoir was the friend's choice. It was heaving when they arrived, which annoyed Roisin, although looking back she's not sure why.

Roisin had a rising feeling of panic in her belly the whole day. She'd left her phone at home – she and Eve were having some stupid argument and Roisin had tossed the phone onto her bedroom floor in a fit of rage and left it there. She remembers how it looked on the uneven wooden boards, flashing at her angrily. Roisin doesn't remember what they ate that day, or whether or not they swam, or if the sky had turned pink by the time they left.

But she does remember that Cal spilt beer all down his front and had to rinse his t-shirt in the loch. They built a contraption of sorts out of driftwood, a tripod which arched over the fire and on which they hung his soaking top like a flag in an attempt to dry it. It worked, but they went for a walk around the loch, and when they returned the driftwood had tumbled into the fire and the polyester t-shirt had melted like a birthday candle onto the hot embers. Black smoke billowed from the flames in hot gasping breaths. Cal was distraught, and then furious with them for finding it so funny, and Roisin's chest lightened a little as she laughed, his anger only making the whole thing funnier. Roisin gave him her purple cardigan, which he wore sulkily in the car home. Roisin hasn't thought about the friend in a long time. There are so many people like that now. People whom she has known intimately, briefly, and then who are gone.

Darkness has begun to creep over the loch. When Roisin turns back to look at Claire, she has disappeared, and so has Eve. She follows the glow of the fire as she wades through the shallows towards the shore. The reservoir has fallen quiet; there is only the occasional hoot from an invisible owl and a murmur of voices from the shore.

Everyone is huddled around the flames. They are all eating out of various vessels: a Tupperware container, a mug. Some are spooning curry straight out of the brass pot which sits on a barbecue grate above Roisin's fire.

The wee boy is fast asleep at a young woman's feet. She strokes his sticky cheek gently, and Roisin watches as she takes off her jacket and carefully covers him with it.

Eve sits next to Claire, who is tucking a towel around her shoulders. Her boyfriend is on the other side of the fire. He is next to a peculiarly gaunt woman with a very wide face. He is leaning over her, one hand on her thigh, to converse passionately with a man Roisin thinks is named Razz on her other side. The woman's eyes are closed, and her face is tilted up to the sky. She looks as though she might be asleep.

As Roisin reaches them, Eve passes her a towel from her bag. Roisin thanks her and starts scrubbing at her hair with the rough fabric.

Roisin sits down beside Eve. She is frozen stiff from the reservoir: icy water droplets are running down her back, and as she moves closer to the fire she is hit with a bright, burning heat. Eve's skin is shining orange from the glow of the flames, and the whole sensation is so overwhelming Roisin feels feverish.

Claire is winding a short piece of leather which looks as though it might be a bracelet round and round her lean fingers. Eve watches her in silence.

The mood is contemplative. Everyone is eating steadily or speaking in hushed tones to those closest to them.

Roisin wraps herself up in the scrubby towel and leans closer to the fire. She is cold and hungry. Nobody has offered her any food, and she doesn't want to ask. She doesn't feel as though she should have to ask. Her wet costume is sticking to her uncomfortably, but she doesn't want to undress in front of all these people so

APRIL

she just pulls a jumper and shorts on top. She fishes her phone out of her trainer and turns it on to check her messages. She has one bar of signal and one text from Calum, asking when she'll be back. She ignores it and puts her phone back into her shoe.

A man is going around the group offering cans of beer. Roisin takes one and smiles at him. Eve declines, and Claire waves him away too.

'I can't, I'm not drinking tonight, I'm driving.'

She pulls her jacket tighter around her shoulders. The man moves on, but Roisin fixes her eyes on Claire, who is holding herself very stiffly, looking directly at the fire.

Roisin isn't sure why she didn't clock earlier that Claire was lying about not being able to drive her to work, but of course Claire isn't drinking. Someone needs to be sober to drive them all back.

For a brief moment Roisin considers saying something, something melodramatic and accusatory.

'Yeah good point, should we start making a move?' Eve says.

'Yes, probably,' Claire says.

'Okay, I'm going to run for a wee, and I'll meet you at the car.'

Eve grabs her shoes and clothes and heads for the woods. Her boyfriend is still talking to Razz, but at a word from Claire he clasps his hand briefly, and gets to his feet. He pulls his jacket over his head and slips on his sandals, then follows Eve into the woods, leaving the two women to collect the rest of the things.

There isn't too much left – they're leaving the firewood and the booze for the people who are staying here. The dusk makes it hard to see; Claire and Roisin use their phone torches to scan the pebbled shore for discarded items.

'Have you got the car keys?' Roisin asks.

'Of course I've got the car keys.'

They continue looking in silence.

'Is there much point looking for shit? Nobody brought anything valuable.'

'Probably not, actually.' Claire sighs and sits down on a rock. Roisin finds herself much taller than Claire; she looms over her awkwardly in the fading light.

'Roisin?' she says.

'Yes?'

'I'm sorry about your job.'

'Oh,' Roisin says. 'That's okay.'

Claire doesn't look sorry. She looks Roisin up and down and then up again and then she stands up. It reminds Roisin of how a snake stretches out alongside their prey.

Claire rakes her hair back from her head, then says, 'Listen, it might not be what you're looking for, but you could come and work for me? It's terrible pay,

APRIL

but I need someone to help me with my new business. And you know, I think Greg could do with some secretarial help too.'

'Greg?'

'My partner.'

Roisin has never heard his name in her life.

'Ah right, Greg. Of course, sorry.'

'Yeah well,' she says. 'Let me know. You can pretty much start whenever, and you know, you can sort out your own hours or whatever you want.'

'That's really nice of you, Claire, thanks. I'll let you know.'

She nods and waves her hand, throws the rucksack over her shoulder and heads up, towards the car. She is barefoot, holding her sandals in her right hand. She steps confidently over the sharp gravelly shore.

Roisin is unsure what to make of this proposition. Maybe Claire is just crap at showing emotions but really feels guilty for lying. Or feels somehow responsible.

Roisin hesitates for a moment before she follows her, looking back at the cool, jet-black loch. It moves as though it is breathing, in and out in cold gasps onto the shore. There is something glittering by the waves.

Roisin picks her way down over the pebbles towards it. It's the anklet Claire gave Eve. It must have slipped off. She picks it up. The metal is cold, and slick from the water. She turns away from the reservoir to walk up the beach to the car.

Before she reaches the others, Roisin pockets the anklet.

A pale silver moon watches, hanging in the last of the gloaming like a pearl dropped in deep purple ink.

*

Roisin wakes up with a jolt because she is choking on Eve's hair. She yanks the sticky strands out, coughing desperately. Incredibly, Eve does not wake up. Roisin falls to her knees onto the floor, breathing heavily. The room is bright with the sun. They must have slept in.

The drive back was quiet and sleepy, the drone of the car the only noise in the still night. Eve and her boyfriend fell asleep on each other in the backseat within minutes. Roisin sat up front next to Claire and tried to remove her wet costume without flashing anyone. That accomplished, Roisin sat back and watched Claire's tattooed hands flex as she changed gears, looking away quickly whenever Claire glanced over to her. Carved into the back of Claire's hand rests a small snake, curled up around a moon. As she moved her hands, the snake moved too.

Roisin made two very quiet cups of tea for Eve and her when they got into the flat, with the intention of doing their usual breakdown of the night's gossip before they passed out, but they barely spoke and didn't touch the tea. Instead they fell asleep on her sofa together, fully clothed, impossibly close.

The two mugs are still on the coffee table now, stone-cold and heavy. Eve's phone sits next to them. Roisin picks it up; Eve has seven missed calls from her boyfriend. This feels to Roisin a bit overkill, it's only midday.

Roisin stands and grabs the mugs, then heads through to the kitchen, leaving Eve. Her throat is scratchy from Eve's hair, and her head is aching. The smell of woodsmoke from the bonfire still clings to her – every inhale tinged with the scent. Roisin feels heavy, hungover.

Cal is in the kitchen. He is reading, legs crossed, at the kitchen table. There is a small pot of tea in front of him. Roisin thinks, underneath her own stench, that she can smell camomile. Roisin wonders hopefully if Cal noticed that she didn't sleep in her own room.

'Morning,' Roisin says, crossing over towards the sink. She pours the two mugs of tea down the drain and leaves the dirty cups on the side for Cal to do later.

'Morning,' Cal says.

It's another hot day. The kitchen feels like a greenhouse; the sun is beating down in through the large window.

Eve has put her rhododendron on the wide windowsill. It looks particularly beautiful in the light. Roisin has to push its leaves to the side to reach the pot of normal teabags. Cal has delicately arranged his porcelain kettle, loose-leaf teas and favourite mugs without much thought for practicalities.

Roisin turns to look at Cal. He has put too much gel in his hair. A lank curl is sticking to his forehead. He is not paying any attention to her.

The kettle rumbles loudly, steam coming out of the top and clouding the window. Roisin can see it curl around the ghost of a smiley face one of them must have etched in the glass. Her head is throbbing. The sound of the kettle is grinding against her forehead. Impatient, she clicks it off early and pours the water into the mug. The teabag floats limply in the water; it clearly wasn't hot enough.

She goes to open the fridge and, as she has been doing since she lost her job, steals Cal's milk. He is too engrossed in his book to notice, which is good because he caught her doing it last week too and she panicked and told him she's stopped buying it because she's trying to go vegan. This obviously made no sense, but he didn't seem to care. Or he pretended not to. Cal can be nice like that.

The milk makes the tea look even worse: anaemic and slimy. Roisin decides that it can't be that bad and will probably help her throat, so she moves over to the table and sits with both elbows firmly on the wood and sips her tea. It is pretty horrible. She thinks there might still be a hair stuck in her throat.

They sit in silence for a while. The kitchen is bright with hot light and a bead of sweat trickles down Roisin's back. It itches.

The sofa is too small for two people to sleep on. All of last night Roisin thought she was going to fall off it. Roisin waited until she heard Eve's breath get steady against the back of her neck and then reached out her arm really slowly and pulled the coffee table towards her, inch by inch so she wouldn't wake Eve, until it was close enough that she could shift her legs onto it.

Roisin didn't really sleep. She woke up every hour or so in the exact same position, terrified to move in case she woke Eve. The anklet was still in the pocket of her shorts, and she could feel the sofa pressing the metal hard against her waist.

She didn't dream, but the first time she woke she thought that she'd dreamt the whole trip. The image of Eve floating in the loch was burned into her eyelids like she'd stared too hard at the bonfire.

TWO: MAY

ROISIN IS LYING ON the sofa. Eve is kneeling next to her, face so close Roisin can smell her stale breath. There is a greasy man Roisin remembers being much older than her in secondary school sitting in her living room.

His name is Mark. Roisin didn't realise he and Eve were still in touch until he turned up at her door yesterday with twelve cans of Strongbow Dark Fruits and a rucksack. She hasn't seen him since she was a teenager and he was in his mid to late twenties and hung around outside the school gates like an angel of death.

He looks identical now. He's wearing a tripper jumper and cargo trousers and hasn't tied his shoelaces. He looks like the sort of person you would stay away from in a supermarket but whom you might approach to ask for directions at Doune the Rabbit Hole. Everyone is draped over the furniture, all still rough from last night when they relived their wasted youth by sitting on the floor, getting stoned and drinking until their heads got thick and fuzzy.

Cal smashed their last wine glass. He was steaming, gesticulating too energetically while ranting about how it's anti-Scottish bias that they're upping the price of alcohol. Nobody had the sense or willpower to clean up the mess, so they just avoided the sofa. Roisin said it looked like glass sharks were sticking out of the deep blue sea, but nobody seemed to be very interested in this. Roisin and Cal fell asleep top to toe like children under the coffee table to the hum of the CD player turned low while Eve and Mark fondled each other underneath a blanket on the other side of the room.

'Stop blinking,' Eve says. Roisin fixes her gaze at a point on the ceiling where the paper is peeling away.

Eve is trying to paint her face. Fuck knows why this is Eve's preferred position, but she told Roisin to lie down so she did. Cal and Mark are silent. They both look fucked up. Cal's skin is a pale shade of grey, and Roisin watched him sneak sugar into his tea. He ate four fried eggs for breakfast, smeared bloody with ketchup.

Eve has clearly noticed the atmosphere of her party is no longer what she had intended. Her eyes are wide, and she keeps talking nervously to no response. She invited lots of people, Roisin knows. Mark is the only one who has turned up.

It is Beltane tonight. This is what has prompted Mark's pilgrimage. Eve must have invited him personally. Roisin can't understand why he would be friends with anyone Eve is friends with now. He and his friends take mushrooms in their mums' back gardens rather than ayahuasca in yurts. But an invitation from someone like Eve, Roisin thinks, would be more than enough to drag him from his pit.

Eve has one hand firmly on Roisin's shoulder while the other hand paints swirls in delicate but deliberate motions up and over her face. She shifts into a cross-legged position, then, unsatisfied, she gets up and kneels on the sofa instead, squashing Roisin's legs against the back cushions. Roisin can feel Eve's hips relax into her. She puts her hand back on Roisin's shoulder and leans over her, examining her painted face. Eve's fingers are soft, her nail polish chipped.

There is an oval shaped bruise at the base of Eve's neck, soft green with age.

Eve's hand loosens its grip on Roisin's shoulder. She pulls back and surveys her work. Roisin can't look her in the eye.

'Okay, I think you're done!' Eve exclaims. She grabs a hand mirror from the coffee table and holds it up to Roisin's face.

It takes Roisin a moment to recognise herself. Eve has pasted white over her entire face and down part of her neck too, so that her brown eyes almost look black. She has blended blues and greens in psychedelic spirals across Roisin's cheeks and up over her forehead but has left her eyes completely clear of makeup, so that it gives the appearance that she is wearing a circus mask. Her lips are painted white. Roisin wonders if she will be able to talk. She wonders if Eve has pasted her lips right shut so that she will never talk again.

'Class,' Roisin says, shifting up onto her elbows.

'Who's next?' Eve says.

*

They end up being late. Claire finally replied to Eve's insistent texting to tell her that the procession had already left by the time they did. It is not nearly as warm as they had predicted it would be (so much for the fucking heatwave) and so Eve and Roisin are both wearing clothes which are deeply inappropriate for the weather. Eve has at least brought a thick black velvet cloak she borrowed especially for the occasion from a friend who does the ghost tours on the Royal Mile. Roisin is wearing her old denim jacket over an outfit she borrowed from Eve.

Roisin glares jealously at the men. Mark and Cal

MAY

are wrapped in layers of thick warm fabric, bundled up tightly as they face the drizzle and the harsh wind, stomping through the muddy track up the hill through London Road Gardens.

Roisin's fingers are so cold they hurt, and her face is numb. She has an ache in her stomach where food should be. Cal hasn't been food shopping this week yet. Eve strides out in front of the group; she is laughing and flirting with some American Beltane tourists who asked them for directions to Calton Hill. Roisin can't understand how she isn't hungry and miserable.

The sky is a deep steel grey, and although Eve and her new friends are visible up ahead, talking energetically, Roisin can't hear them at all. The wind is whipping all the sound away into the air.

Mark, Cal and Roisin drag along behind Eve and her new pals. Roisin is pleasantly surprised that Cal came, although she can tell he wants to go back to the flat, get into bed and watch *Hollyoaks*. He sat pretty much in silence while everyone got ready, but he did let Eve paint his face in swirls of pink and red.

Roisin falls into step with Mark, who seems to be half-heartedly trying to catch up with Eve. As they walk together, he avoids looking at Roisin and glances back at Cal every now and then desperately, as though willing another man to be near him.

Bizarrely, it reminds Roisin of how women behave

when they're walking home alone at night; separately but together, poised against a threat that might appear at any moment. Except, Roisin thinks, he's scared of being told to fuck off, rather than being raped and dismembered in a park.

Roisin does not remember Mark being this short. But, now that she thinks of it, she's not sure she was fully done growing when she last saw him. Roisin is not uncomfortable around Mark, but he seems to very much be uncomfortable around her. Roisin asks him how he's enjoying Edinburgh, and he looks at her with wide, frozen eyes. He doesn't bother responding, and they continue traipsing up the hill.

Odd groups of people swarm past them, racing either to or from the hill. There's a skinny boy stood in the middle of the road with his phone out and up, searching for signal. He sways slightly, eyes unfocused. Two young girls wearing matching ripped jeans with fishnets underneath are asking him what his name is, whereabouts does he stay, and if they can walk him home, because they think he's taken it a wee bit too far.

Eve is waiting for them at the top of the path, below the observatory.

Her arms are opened wide so that the black velvet cloak spills from them like water. Her head is turned up towards the sky. Mouth open, she is catching drops

MAY

on her tongue like she has never seen rain before.

She looks down at them panting, then waves for them to hurry up. By the time they reach the top of the hill, Eve and her new friends have vanished into the fray. Roisin can't conjure up the energy to be pissed off.

It's chaos. The faces of the people flicker in and out of Roisin's vision. There seems to be a heat emanating off of them. The noise pulses around her like she's in a club. Roisin turns out to look over the city and tries to breathe for a moment through the sight of the sky and sea, but the fog is so thick and muddy brown that she can only see as far as the edge. And actually, she's not sure it is the edge, the cloud keeps shifting, and really, the edge could be anywhere.

For a moment she considers how dangerous it might be, being up here in this weather, steaming, surrounded by similarly trashed strangers, but then the thrum of the music makes her turn her head, and the dancers weave in and out of the crowds in swift motions, pulling her attention back to the small pocket of land they are standing on, and to the sound of the frantic drumbeat which pulls the crowds to and fro in a trance.

Mark nudges Roisin. He proffers a Fanta bottle filled with brown liquid and a small round pill. She takes both, not necessarily because she wants to, but because it is easier than refusing. The liquid is not only horrible, it's completely unidentifiable. She offers the bottle to Cal, who shakes his head and grimaces.

She takes out her phone and checks to see if she has any messages from Eve. There's instead a text from Claire, telling them to head to the north side of the monument – they've got a really good view.

Roisin takes another drink from the bottle and goes to pass it back to Mark, but he's vanished too.

The wind has whipped up the rain into tiny bullets. She and Cal stand hunched together, braced against it. Making a decision, Roisin starts to drag him towards the fray, telling him that Claire says she's over by the monument.

'Nae chance,' he says, digging his heels in.

He looks like a dog that has been left out in the rain, deflated. His pointed nose is bright red at the tip.

'Wise up, it'll be warmer in the crowd,' Roisin tells him, and she marches along the gravel path without him. After a few steps she hears him crunching behind her. He loops his arm into hers, and they push through the hoards together.

When they get over to the monument, they spot Claire easily. She is dressed all in bright red: a thick, cherry-coloured dress with a knitted hat tied around her chin. The noise from the drums is overwhelming here. It reverberates around Roisin's head.

MAY

Roisin throws her arms around Claire, who pulls back a little, smiling awkwardly. She smells familiar to Roisin, like sandalwood and something she can't quite place.

She introduces Cal, and he puts his hand up in a hello. Claire nods at him, then pulls Roisin closer to ask where Eve is. Claire's breath is warm against the soft skin beneath Roisin's ear. Roisin scans the crowd. Everyone is blurring together in a lovely haze. When Roisin moves her head to the side she feels like she's floating, so she does it again and again.

They stand there in silence for a long time, and Roisin lets her hands go cold and stiff and her face go warm from the rocking of the drums.

There is a beautiful queen in the clearing in front of the monument. It is the woman who lives across the road. Roisin realises she is the most beautiful woman in the world. The most beautiful, she says, moving her lips emptily like a fish. The woman is not smoking, she is dressed all in white and stars spiral from her outstretched hands. A man covered in leaves prowls before her.

Roisin can see Mark and Eve above her. They are on the sofa together, covered in broken glass, their faces flickering as they tangle like snakes around and around, lips touching, breath flowing as they float through the waves and out to sea.

Roisin is sitting on the wet hard ground and Claire and Cal are kneeling in front of her.

The queen bows down to the trees, and they are set ablaze. Roisin opens her eyes as wide as she can, and she lets the fire burn into the back of her skull.

Claire's hair feels soft and warm underneath her hat. She is silhouetted in deep blue against the burnt orange fire raging behind her.

And then the crowd gets very very quiet, and all Roisin can hear is a rushing in her ears and a slight whining, and she thinks that maybe she should have eaten today, and it's then that she throws up on Claire's cherry-red dress.

*

Even though her bedroom is tiny, the best thing about it is that Roisin essentially gets two rooms. The first is the one you walk into, about the same width as a single bed and maybe a metre longer, and the second is above it. If she walks to the end of the room towards the window and climbs up the ladder which is nailed to the left-hand wall, she can crawl into her bed. It's got just enough head space to sit up straight in. She has complete privacy in there.

That's why she's been keeping the anklet Claire gave Eve up there. She should probably have returned

MAY

it to Eve that night at the reservoir, but the weight of it in her pocket on the drive home felt like it was tethering Roisin to Eve, keeping her feet firmly on the ground. She's liked knowing that it's up there. Eve asked if anyone had seen it the morning after the trip, but after a brief search of the flat she concluded that it must have fallen off when she went swimming. This was true, so Roisin didn't feel the need to correct her.

When Roisin gets home from Beltane she reaches under her pillow and pulls out Eve's heavy silver anklet from where it is wrapped up in one of Eve's pyjama t-shirts. It's cool on her fingers, and when she pokes out her tongue it's cool on that too. It has tiny bells on it which jangle softly if moved too quickly or too energetically. Roisin wonders how much it costs. If she were Claire, with all that money, she thinks she'd probably buy beautiful women pretty things too. She falls asleep holding it to her chest.

When she wakes in the morning the anklet is still clenched in her fist. She wraps it up in the soft t-shirt and places it gently back under her pillow.

Roisin climbs down the steps, pulls on a hoodie and pads through to the living room. Eve is lying on the bare wooden floor, naked blue-cold limbs tangled up with Mark's.

She stands there for a moment. They are like that picture of John and Yoko. Roisin remembers how short he seemed last night. Now Eve looks too small for him.

They ended up in Claire's house last night, Cal and Roisin. She gave Roisin a glass of water and made her a cup of tea while she put her soiled dress in the wash, and then she asked Roisin about the job again. Too tired to resist, Roisin agreed to come round on Tuesday. When they finally managed to escape, Cal started laughing hysterically, saying, 'It's the sign of a terrible night when you end up in Stockbridge. Where d'you get chips from in fuckin Stockbridge?'

There was a very fine rain falling in the glare of the streetlamps. It collected in a mist around Cal's head, glowing gently yellow in the streetlights like bioluminescent algae, and when Roisin reached up and touched her hair it was damp too.

Eve has put her phone on top of a stack of books which are propping open the door. Roisin picks the books up and softly closes the light wooden door behind her.

The books are mostly Cal's – churned-out sci-fi paperbacks. Roisin picks up Eve's phone, leans against the radiator and presses the middle button. It lights up. When it asks her for the password she types in Eve's birthday, and it lets her in immediately.

There is mumbling coming from the living room.

MAY

Eve is groaning, clearly waking up. Roisin holds still, and she falls quiet.

Her notes app is full of fragments of bad poetry.

Her texts are mostly banal and mostly to Roisin, actually, which makes Roisin feel important. Eve's most recent photographs are all nudes. She goes to click back to the home page – this feels like one too many boundaries crossed – but something about them makes her stop.

She is taken aback by how unflattering they are. Eve hasn't contorted herself at all in them: it's as though they were taken in order to prove to herself that she exists, that this is how her body looks, rather than to prove that she was beautiful once, that someone desired her once. Her pale eyes glare at the camera.

Roisin flicks through the photographs one by one – through days and days documented in flat whites, mirror selfies and Edinburgh skylines – until she comes to a screenshot of Google Maps. It's a route leading from Roisin's flat. The time in the corner of the screen reads 01:48.

Before Roisin can look closer at the address on the map, Eve gets a text and she jumps. It's from Eve's boyfriend, asking her where she went. Roisin clicks out of her photos and puts her phone back on top of the pile of books.

Roisin didn't wash her face last night. The mirror

on the wall across the hallway shows a ghoul painted in shades of white and blue. Her dark eyes are watching her.

*

Roisin should probably be more nervous than she is about starting work for Claire. She thinks she's been preoccupied, to be honest. It's hard work being unemployed. Finding something to fill each day is a real chore, it turns out. Especially when you're trying not to spend money at cafés or anything. There's only so many times you can go to the Chamber Street Museum, especially when you're not five. Roisin has started to join Cal in his nightly *Love Island* viewings, and recently it has been the most exciting part of her day. She will admit though that it is a relief to not have to spend any more time at the library printing out CVs or trawling through Indeed. Every now and then she opens up the webpages for the schemes and internships she'd been so determined to get into after uni, but writing an application seemed like an insurmountable task when she knew the place would go to someone who'd spent their summers interning for free somewhere that didn't even have an application process. What was the point, when she could work for a friend? Even if the friend was more of a friend of a

MAY

friend really and she actually was a bit scared of her.

Eve has been staying at her boyfriend's since Beltane. Mark left early the morning after; Roisin didn't get a chance to talk to him really. Eve hasn't said anything to her about the night, which pissed her off. But then, Roisin supposes that it wouldn't have pissed her off if she hadn't known what she'd done, and she's not supposed to know what she's done so she supposes, really, that she has no right to be pissed off.

Eve doesn't know what happened with Claire either. She doesn't know that Roisin went back to her house. She never asked.

It feels private to Roisin, honestly. Claire's home was achingly personal. Roisin isn't sure that she should have been allowed to see her slippers underneath the armchair where she must have discarded them to pull her feet up under her one night. Or to touch the soft orange sofa, which she most probably has slept on. Or the dish full of silver rings on the fireplace. It feels as though by going round Roisin has broken some secret code between them all so that now it is Claire and Roisin and Eve instead of Eve and Claire and Roisin.

Cal, Roisin supposes, saw it all too. But he spent most of his time in the bathroom, probably trying out different soaps and hand creams. Roisin bets Claire's the sort of person to have a hundred little jars of potions and lotions. She does have nice hands.

Perhaps this is why Roisin is not nervous about starting work, because she has already been to Claire's house. Or perhaps it's because she hasn't been able to stop thinking about Eve and Mark.

It's not that he was terrible when they were teenagers: it was fun and exciting to be surrounded by him and his pals, older people who would treat her like she was special and funny the way her peers didn't. She could drink as much as she liked, smoke as much as she liked and then lie on the floor of a dingy flat and stare at the swirls of the ceiling paint until they merged into an image of something better, somewhere better than here.

Or, occasionally, until they merged into the *Trainspotting* baby and Roisin threw up into a stranger's hands and passed out on the carpet until she had to go to school, crusty and stinking, to take notes on Carol Ann Duffy's 'War Photographer'.

Eve bought a new rhododendron the morning after Beltane. Or maybe it's an azalea – Roisin doesn't really know the difference, but this one is smaller, much smaller than her other one. It has no flowers, and it sits in a blue plant pot which is decorated with swipes of green glaze. Eve hasn't been here in days, so it's starting to wilt.

Roisin doesn't want Eve and Mark to get together, but she also doesn't want Eve and her boyfriend to stay

MAY

together. Roisin doesn't know what she wants.

Eve left her things all over the floor of the living room. It's strange: Cal and Roisin haven't been using it since Eve's been gone. They watch *Love Island* uncomfortably at the kitchen table. The living room has been kept like a memorial to her. He'd never admit it, but Roisin thinks that he misses her. It's so quiet there without her.

Roisin tiptoed over the debris this morning to use Eve's mirror. It felt like trespassing. She spent an hour in there trying on different outfits before settling on a t-shirt and jeans. She didn't really know what to wear to this job because she doesn't know what it is.

'How can you not know whit the job is?'

Cal is making Roisin a cup of tea while she pulls on her trainers.

'I dunno – she never really said. I think she mentioned admin work.'

He looks at her incredulously. 'D'you even know whit you're gonna get paid?' he asks, offering her the tea in a pink mug shaped like a boob.

She shrugs. How do you ask a friend of a friend what they're going to pay you for a job you don't know the name of?

'I dunno, but it'll get worked out, don't worry.'

'A still think you should have gone and asked for

your old job back. Don't mix business and family, you know.'

'Claire's not family,' she says, confused.

'Aye, but it's a bit weird isn't it, with Eve and Ian and Claire and then you . . .'

Roisin sits with this sentence for a moment, trying to figure out if she's misheard him.

'Cal, who the fuck is Ian?' she asks.

He looks at Roisin, confused.

'Eve's boyfriend,' he says.

'Eve's boyfriend is called Fraser,' Roisin says. 'Where did you get Ian from?'

'Whit?' he says. 'No he's not. He's called Ian.'

'Calum,' Roisin says, 'what the actual fuck are you talking about. His name's Fraser.'

A seed of doubt is starting to creep into her mind. She was introduced to him at a big gathering; maybe she got confused.

She remembers that he and Eve were still in the talking stage, and he'd said that he wanted to meet her and why didn't they come over to his flat and hang out before he had some of his friends over.

They arrived fifteen minutes after the time he'd said to come. They sat in a nearby café and nursed coffees for nearly forty-five minutes because Eve said that if they showed up early it would be *needy*. This was apparently the worst thing they could be.

MAY

When he'd said *flat*, he was being so modest it was basically a lie. He lived in a terraced townhouse in Morningside. The brick was scrubbed clean of smog, and his door was painted dark blue. There were Tibetan prayer flags wrapped around the railings on the stairs leading up to the door, sodden from the rain. As Roisin walked up the steps in her scuzzy trainers, she felt too poor to even be on the street.

It was at that same party that Eve told Roisin that Fraser or Ian or whatever the fuck his name is didn't believe in penetrative sex. He'd met a guru in Southeast Asia who had told him that vulvas were dirty and should only come into contact with a man's penis when a man wanted to conceive a child.

'So I just suck him off.'

They were in the garden lying top to toe in the hammock strung between two oaks.

'What was the guru called?' Roisin asked her.

'Steve.'

'Steve?'

'Yeah, Steve.'

They were high, and neither of them bothered keeping their voices down as they laughed. The hammock jolted, and they were thrown with a start onto the grass. It took Roisin longer than normal to realise she was on the ground, fuzzy edges lifting from the sides of her eyes.

'D'you think we can ask Eve her boyfriend's name after knowin him fir three months?' Cal asks.

'Ehhh . . . probably not,' Roisin says. 'Is Claire even called Claire?'

'Aye, definitely. *Claire* is Eve's favourite word,' says Cal, downing the last dregs of his tea and pulling his backpack on.

*

It is only when Roisin gets to Stockbridge that she realises she doesn't have Claire's address and the only time she's ever been there she was trashed. Roisin sends her a text and darts into a café, grudgingly paying £3.50 in change she scooped from the bottom of Cal's backpack for the privilege of a bitter coffee drunk quickly on a plastic chair on the pavement.

It's a beautiful day; Roisin thinks the heatwave they were promised might be beginning to take hold again. Summer in Scotland is like nothing else. Roisin once knew a girl from California who told her that Scotland becomes a different country when the weather is good – that you don't realise how miserable people are here most of the time until it's summer and you remember what happiness looks like.

Roisin thinks in hindsight that she probably should

have taken offence at this, but the girl was right. It's not yet 9 a.m., and it's a Tuesday, but because it's not cloudy and it's maybe 15 degrees out, people are happy. Two skinny guys in grey Adidas jersey shorts have just walked past her, shirtless and grinning, looking like the cats who got the cream.

Roisin's phone lights up – Claire with her address. Serendipitously, it's not far from where she chose to stop. She chugs the last dregs of the coffee and wanders up the street.

Claire answers the door in dark red dungarees, with her hair piled on top of her head in a scrunchie. It's still wet; a bead of water is rolling slowly down her forehead.

Claire asks her to take her shoes off then leads her down the stairs into the kitchen, where a steaming French press and two squat mugs sit waiting. She has decanted milk into a small brown jug.

The house looks different in the daylight, bigger. The kitchen/living room is open-plan – the kitchen has large French doors, which are flung open onto the patio garden. Everything is a warm shade of orange, red or brown. The pale wooden table runs parallel to the sink and countertop, above which are long shelves stacked with glass jars filled with dried pulses, rice and pasta.

She pours Roisin a coffee and puts a plate of sliced

apple on the table. She apologises for not having any biscuits or anything.

'I've just been taking some time to purge my body of all that crap,' she says, gesturing into thin air. Roisin nods, wondering if by *crap* she means *food*.

They sit in weighty silence for a while, drinking slowly.

'So,' Claire says finally. 'Where would you like to start?'

Roisin's not very sure how Claire wants her to respond to this question as Claire still hasn't told her exactly what it is she wants her to do. What Roisin really wants to ask Claire is how much she's going to pay her, and when.

Roisin takes a long sip of coffee. 'Up to you,' she says.

'Well, I suppose you can start with the computer stuff – I need a website.'

Roisin nods. Claire stands up and leads her back up the stairs. Roisin's heart is racing – the two coffees are making her jittery. She has to hold onto the banister tightly.

Roisin hasn't eaten properly for a couple of days now because she hasn't been able to afford to do a big shop at the supermarket and Cal keeps buying shit she doesn't like. She might be skint, but she at least has the dignity to not nick fig rolls and frozen broccoli.

MAY

She's been living off of Lidl penne pasta and tinned tomatoes on toast, but it's getting to the point where she's not sure she can stomach them for much longer. Eve hasn't been around, but even if she had been it wouldn't have made Roisin's life easier: she either doesn't eat, or she eats out.

To get to Claire's study you have to go through her bedroom. It must be just her bedroom because although Roisin knows Claire is married there is no sign of her husband anywhere in the house. The bedsheets are a pale red, and there is only one bedside table. On it is a hardback book, a small lamp, a hairbrush and a dish with some silver coins. There are only women's clothes hanging on the clothes rail, and only women's shoes beneath it.

Claire sets Roisin up with the computer, explains what she wants in a website, and Roisin spends the majority of the day fiddling with fonts on WordPress and combing through her desk drawers (not much of interest – mostly pens and loose papers).

Claire has, however, left her diary splayed open on the desk like the morning paper. On today's date she has written *Roisin*. The rest of the week is completely empty. Roisin flips the pages back: last week she went to yoga at 11 a.m. on Tuesday. And nothing else. As she flips further back into the book she finds not very much at all.

The house is so quiet. Does she spend every day here, like this? Roisin doesn't know what Claire is doing downstairs, but it can't be much or she'd hear her: the walls are so thin Roisin heard her pouring out food for the cat in the kitchen.

Roisin flips the pages looking for any sign of her husband, a date pencilled in or a trip to Glasgow or even just his name anywhere. *Greg – dentist* maybe. But there is nothing.

When Roisin goes through to her room, padding especially quietly in her socks, she opens the chest of drawers and lifts up Claire's underwear, her linen trousers, her makeup bag, looking for evidence that he has ever existed in this space. Nothing.

Dissatisfied, she goes back to WordPress.

Claire interrupts her a few hours later to let her know she's made tea, and they head downstairs to sit and drink together.

Roisin is surprised by how different Claire is in her own home. She always had an image of her as straight-backed and barbed. Now though, her soft eyes watch Roisin's hands as Roisin pours herself tea. Claire's posture is crooked, she sits with one leg under the other, and she has on odd socks.

'So,' Roisin says. 'What made you want to be a reiki masseuse or whatever?'

Claire looks at her. 'I know you think it's stupid,' she

says. 'But it helped me. And people will pay a fortune for it.'

'No, no,' Roisin says, flustered. 'I don't think it's stupid.'

Roisin does think it's stupid. But she feels bad for being so flippant. She didn't realise she had the power to disarm her like that.

'It's just a really healing practice,' Claire tells her, leaning in across the table. 'I can show you if you'd like.'

Roisin starts to say no, thank you, but Claire has already taken her hand in hers. They are warm and soft. Her hair has escaped its scrunchie and is falling into her face.

She tells Roisin to close her eyes, and Roisin sits in her chair and tries to stay very still. She's thinking about how much she'd like to be the sort of person who decants their bags of pasta into a glass jar so that it looks like it appeared out of nowhere when she feels Claire's hot sweet breath on the nape of her neck.

It's then that she kisses her.

THREE: JUNE

TODAY IS A THURSDAY near the end of June, and Roisin is sitting in a bar off Nicolson Street sipping at a glass of wine and waiting for the clock to turn half past ten so that she can send Eve a *where are you* text.

That afternoon she went to get her hair cut. She runs her hand over the shorn bristles at the back of her head. The hairdresser gave her a massage, and she can still feel her head tingling. Roisin is not yet used to being able to do what she wants, when she wants it. She just called them up and booked it. She got given a latte while the hairdresser chopped and massaged and berated her for washing her hair every day. When she came out she felt lighter, and two girls on the street met her eye in that way they do sometimes that means *I see you.*

The bar is full of people who look like Roisin. Like art students with nicotine addictions. She watches them now, heads tilted towards lovers or friends, long scarves and clunky boots trailing along the sticky floor. Roisin pulls nervously at a strand of hair the hairdresser left long by mistake. She is very aware of being alone. She managed to claim a table, and the three empty chairs seem to her to be extremely visible, the lack of people glaringly obvious in the packed, sweaty room. Once Eve gets here, it'll be better. Roisin's been spending so much time either with Eve or with Claire recently that it's felt bizarre today to be by herself. She felt sick when Eve left last night to go to her boyfriend's.

This morning, Roisin sat in the living room on Eve's sofa and stared at the long branch of the tree outside which has been creeping its fingers closer and closer all year so that now it raps on the window with the morning sun, leaves pressed up against the glass as though gasping under a plastic bag. Roisin wondered whether or not she should report the tree as a hazard to the council, so she could get it cut down for more light in the flat. She decided against it, thinking about the reaction if she were found out.

Eve emerges through the crowd like a snake from the bushes and sits down opposite Roisin with an exaggerated sigh.

'It is *so* fucking hot in here,' she says, leaning over to take a large gulp of Roisin's wine. 'Here, okay so, I'm sorry I'm late but there was this mad guy on a soapbox by the uni right, I don't know why the fuck you'd even bother with the Christian shit when there's

JUNE

all those students about who pray to like, a better God or to themselves or whatever. But anyway there was this guy ranting and raving about heaven and hell and how we're all doomed to rot or burn because we have gay sex! I mean, he didn't actually say gay sex but like, it was heavily implied.'

Eve leans forward and takes another large gulp of Roisin's drink. Sweat has pooled in the dip above her lip and her makeup has melted; foundation swirls around blackheads on her nose.

'Anyway, so, what was I saying? Oh yeah, so then there was this other guy, and he was like, not having any of it, and he started arguing with him, talking about like all these famines and stuff that God could have easily avoided but like, didn't and like about how the soapbox guy's definition of *good* was fucked up. But he was being nearly as fucking annoying as the soapbox guy.' The pupils of Eve's eyes are dilated.

'Anyway,' Eve says, 'how are you, how's your day been, I *love* your new haircut!' She peers at Roisin analytically, head tilted. 'Such an interesting style.'

Roisin pulls at the back of her hair. 'Yeah, not too bad,' says Roisin. 'What's the plan tonight?'

'Well,' says Eve, 'I think it'll just be us actually. I thought cans cause this place is fucking extortionate and then we can come back here or go Cowgate later? It's solstice! The night is young, and it will stay young!'

Eve punctuates this remark with a clumsy flourish of Roisin's glass of wine, and Roisin notices two pink dots high on her cheeks.

Roisin forgot about the solstice. She had sort of assumed that this would be a big event, but she's pleased that this isn't the case.

'Cool,' Roisin says. 'D'you want a drink before we head?'

'Nah, I hate it in here, too many students.' Eve drinks all but a dribble of Roisin's wine and then offers Roisin the glass. Roisin shakes her head with a grimace, and Eve downs the rest. They barge through the crowds together and emerge blinking into the pale evening light.

The city is alive. It's buzzing with a kind of energy that's hard to describe, a sort of fizzing so that the edges of the buildings pop and blur into each other as Roisin and Eve meander happily down Nicolson Street. Everyone and their mum seems to be making the most of the daylight. The students are either bleary-eyed and trackie-clad, carrying large rucksacks on their way from or to the library – where they have either been or will stay until the wee hours – or they're fizzing too, bursting with pent-up energy, ready to explode one last time before they are shipped off back down to England.

They go into the Tescos, and with burgeoning pride

JUNE

Roisin buys Eve cans of cloudy cider and a bottle of sweet white wine and two punnets of Aberdeenshire strawberries and packets of Bombay mix and salt and vinegar crisps and hummus and vegan chocolate studded with hazelnuts and strawberry laces and fizzy rainbow belts and rosemary crackers and sundried tomatoes and artichokes in olive oil and ham and cold chicken and taramasalata, whatever the fuck that is, and a carton of eggs for Cal, because he asked her to pick some up.

Roisin doesn't flinch at the till. Roisin hasn't told Eve who she's working for. It's not that she deliberately kept it from her, it's more that Eve tends to control the flow of the conversation most of the time so there never really seemed to be a moment to tell her. When Eve asked where Roisin had been recently, Roisin had told her that she'd got a job. Eve had nodded disinterestedly, and Roisin had decided that there was no point in telling her.

Claire asked Roisin not to tell anyone about them sleeping together anyway, so it made sense to just wrap the whole thing up in a nice secret parcel.

They don't say much to each other, Roisin and Claire.

Roisin turns up for work between nine and half past and Claire gives her a coffee. Then Roisin goes upstairs and slips Claire's expensive skincare items into her backpack and fiddles around with the colour scheme on the Canva logo and waits.

The first couple of times she'd call Roisin down for tea, and they'd sit and sip from the steam in a potent silence until Claire (it was always Claire) reached out and brushed her hand with her fingertips.

Now, though, Roisin waits until she hears her footsteps on the stairs. Claire comes through to her bedroom and sits on the bed and waits.

She paid her for the first time last Friday. Obviously Roisin always knew that she was going to get paid. But when Claire had offered her the job she'd said that the pay would be shit, and what Claire has been paying her is not shit. Not that Roisin is going to question her. It's amazing how much freedom money can give a person. Roisin is beginning to understand how come Eve is so much fun and how come Claire doesn't have a single wrinkle. The biting anxiety at the root of Roisin's spine has dissipated. Having money is like wearing a massive warm blanket all the time.

She bought new clothes! New trainers! No holes! She did a big online shop and bought all her and Cal's favourite foods. But Roisin thinks that maybe her body must have got used to being hungry because now everything turns to glue in her mouth. But at least she can eat, if she wants to.

Most importantly, she and Cal have actually been

JUNE

going out with Eve again instead of just watching telly. They've been going to a different bar every night after they finish work, and last weekend they even went out. Eve's boyfriend turned up randomly – Roisin still doesn't know how he knew where they were. He and Eve had a massive screaming fit in the middle of the dancefloor. Roisin has never seen Cal so uncomfortable. They left almost immediately after that because, despite Cal spewing when they got home, none of them was drunk enough for what they witnessed – sweat poured from the walls like the club itself was alive and this was the beast's stomach, dissolving teenagers in noxious fluids and WKD.

But all that money. It's not irrational to think that Claire might not just be paying Roisin for making her a WordPress. Or Claire could be mental and not understand how much money she's paying her. It could be either. Roisin is surprised by how much she doesn't mind which.

Halfway along North Bridge, Eve breathlessly declares that she can't wait anymore, and rips open a punnet of strawberries. She eats them ravenously, juice bursting out and down the sides of her mouth. She rips the stems off methodically and throws them at her feet. Roisin watches her as she splits the stream of people on the path like the Red Sea. The light behind her filters through her hair.

The moment snaps. There is a scream: sharp and cold and clear. They both turn quickly – they are not sure whether it is the sort of scream that means HELP or the sort of scream that means RUN. The crowd turns with them, all towards the sound. There is a small woman wearing a large waterproof jacket crouched over in the street, rocking backwards and forwards. The crowd seems suspended – unsure whether to move towards her or away from her. She lifts her head to reveal straggly hair, tears tracking marks on her unwashed face. She opens her red mouth and screams 'BIIIIIIITCH'. Everything seems to suddenly root itself back into reality, their feet seem to land back on the ground. The crowd moves as one, away from her. They hear a man say, 'Och, she'll be fine. Saw her yesterday playin the exact same game doon the bottom a Leith Walk. She's a fuckin chancer.'

Eve glowers at him and breaks away from the crowd, moving quickly and determinedly towards the woman. Roisin thinks she recognises her – in fact she definitely does. The man is right, she's normally in Leith. She wonders if that's why everyone has turned away – they all know who she is. Too uncomfortable to help her once and then never again, to meet her eyes with recognition every day as they haul bags of food past her.

Eve has reached the woman. She kneels in front of

her and asks her if she's okay. The woman glowers at Eve and rains insults down on her like hailstones, rising up to her full height – still a head shorter than Eve.

'Fine then, fuck you too!' Eve sticks two fingers up at her and turns, shaking, to march towards Roisin.

'Fuckin hell,' Eve says.

'Alright?' Roisin asks.

Eve shakes her head tightly. It has now become Eve's pain, Eve is the one who needs to be comforted. Eve needs to be cotton-wool-padded against the evil woman who swore at her and reminded her about all the horrible things which happen every day and which she is ignoring.

Roisin is ignoring them too.

'I hate this fuckin city,' Eve says.

Roisin reaches into the plastic shopping bag and pulls out a can of cider. She cracks it open and hands it to Eve wordlessly. Eve laughs wryly and takes it.

They walk in silence the rest of the way. When they emerge from the walled-in path onto the hill it is to find Edinburgh sprawled out below, a giant webbed mess of spun gold buildings glinting in the fading sun.

A breeze whips over them, a cold gasp from the sea, and the warm evening light pools at their feet. Eve and Roisin tuck themselves into a patch of grass near the monument, shielding themselves from the worst of the wind.

The wine is sealed with a cork which quickly proves to be a problem. Eve puts the bottle inside her trainer and rams it against the monument. It doesn't budge. Despairingly, she resorts instead to digging the cork out with Roisin's keys. She extracts most of it, but small pieces of cork float miserably in the wine, and with each swig they both have to spit out tiny lumps.

'It feels a bit desperate, this,' Roisin says.

'Yeah well,' says Eve, 'when we drink it always feels desperate.'

Eve's shoulders are pulled up tight against her ears. It has pissed her off, Roisin can tell, that she didn't get to be the good person. This is something Roisin can understand.

They sit in silence, watching a boat appear to move weightlessly along the Firth in the distance. Roisin feels weightless too, as though she can feel the Earth's axis turning, slowly slowly. Probably, though, it's the wine.

Eve breaks the silence.

'That woman was so fuckin weird. Like, I was trying to help.'

Roisin nods.

'Nobody else was gonna help her out. At least I tried to care, you know?'

Eve emphasises the *nobody else*. Roisin waits. She wants to hear Eve tell her she's better than her. Come on, Roisin thinks, egging her on in her head, be a bitch so I can tell you to fuck off.

Eve takes a deep breath, raising her hands above her head and bringing them down slowly in a stretch.

The walls go back up around her voice, accent shifting south.

'It's fine. It's just like, come on, *I* am not the enemy. *We* are not the enemy.' She motions at Roisin. 'We get it, you know?'

Eve plops a ruby-red sundried tomato in her mouth and chews slowly, then takes a long drag of the wine. She crosses her legs out in front of her and leans back against the sun.

'Claire was like, ranting about something the other day, I don't even remember what, some political thing I can't like, be fucking bothered to keep up with. But she was bitching about it as though it actually affected her.' Roisin bristles a little at Claire's name. She has been trying very hard to not think about Claire. But she is too surprised by Eve's tone to not be curious; Eve doesn't usually speak about Claire with anything other than reverence.

'I had a proper go at her actually,' Eve says, turning to Roisin.

'Oh? How come?'

'I don't know, nothing really. It was stupid. It's just like, hard to be around that lot sometimes, you know?'

Roisin pauses before responding. She doesn't like to think about Claire and Eve being connected in a way that doesn't involve her. Not even to be pissed off at each other.

'Yeah,' Roisin says finally. 'It's shite.'

Roisin drinks the rest of the bottle of wine in one long pull and cracks a cider from the packet. She wants to get so drunk that she can't feel where she stops and the world starts, so drunk that the alcohol will unstitch her consciousness from the web of reality, so that she can lie on the grass and look up at the sky and feel like that is all there is in the world.

Roisin often feels as though she is walking along a craggy cliff's edge, as though the slightest change in wind direction or the shortest, sharpest errant thought could send her flying, make her lose her balance and tumble.

'Why do you hang out with them then? If you hate them so much?' Roisin asks bitterly, popping her cider. It fizzes over the can onto the grass.

'I don't know,' Eve says, not looking at Roisin. 'It's fun, I guess. To get to not be a real person for a bit.' Eve's pale hair obscures her face. The wind can't seem to decide which direction it wants to take.

'Why do you?' Eve asks. There is something accusatory in her tone.

Roisin isn't sure either. At first she just wanted to

eke out her time with Eve as much as possible. Now though, there's not that excuse. Roisin likes feeling as if she has a life outside of Eve, something Eve doesn't know. She likes how it makes her feel when she knows that Claire doesn't want her to leave in the evening. She likes not having to talk about real things, about job applications and the broken toilet. And she liked it when the money dropped into her account as though it was absolutely nothing, like it was a score on a video game. And she likes when Eve tells her about Claire's incredible meditation tip and she gets a hot warm feeling knowing that for a couple of hours every day she gets to make Claire happier than Eve ever has. And she likes knowing that Eve would kill to be in her place.

Before Roisin can think of an answer she can give Eve, Eve's boyfriend shouts up at them both. He's waving from below them with a big rucksack on his back.

'Hey guys,' he says. 'What's up?'

Roisin doesn't understand how he knew they were here.

He bounds up the path and tells them both that they're going to Portobello in a minute: Claire's going to call when she's at the bottom of the hill and Eve wasn't picking up her phone, why wasn't Eve picking up her phone?

They sit and listen to him talk for a while about his

day and all the shops he had to go round before he could find real wine and how the front wheel of his bike got stolen by a junkie and half of Roisin desperately wants to tell him that actually, you shouldn't say that word and the other half desperately wants to tell him that, actually, in Scotland they're *jakies* but she doesn't say either and then Claire calls and he and Eve both stand up to leave, and Roisin says nah, you go ahead, Cal's meeting me here later, which is a lie, but she cannot see Claire and Eve together, not yet.

When Eve stands up to go, the sun silhouettes her. If Roisin was a different kind of person, if Roisin was sentimental or maybe even had just a few more drinks in her she would have said there was a halo behind her head. But Roisin isn't that kind of person, she doesn't think, and Eve is gone before she can try to find out.

Roisin is left alone, the uneaten food and the alcohol splayed out at her feet like a crime scene.

She drinks the rest of the booze methodically, crumpling can after can into the grass, then closes her eyes and lies back on the hill, arms open wide. She feels untethered from the ground, like she is alone in space, an astronaut cut from the ship.

There are no stars. The sun doesn't set. Roisin puts all the food into the bin.

★

JUNE

Roisin is sitting at the kitchen table drinking a cup of tea. Calum made it for her earlier, and she let it go cold. She's had to reheat it in the microwave, but she put it in for too long so when it came out it burnt her tongue. It's Saturday, she slept in until 3 p.m., and she still feels a bit groggy now. She didn't shower when she woke up, and she's regretting it; her hair is clinging limply to her forehead, and she feels a layer of sleep on her body still.

The girl who lives across the road is leaning out of the window. Her hair is tied in a long plait which swings from her neck. Roisin can hear the muffled sounds of a bass beat coming through the panes. The girl is swaying, eyes closed, holding a lit cigarette. Puffs of smoke float up over the tops of the tenement buildings. Her thick purple jumper is too much for the weather. The sun is beating down hard on the bleached white stone of the tenement.

'Roisin? Can I nick your Docs?' Eve's voice rings through from the living room.

She pads through in thick woollen socks and a miniskirt. She is already pulling on Roisin's boots. They're new.

Roisin nods in pointless agreement, and Eve sits at the table next to her and begins lacing them up.

'You're not ready,' Eve says.

Roisin thought she was ready. They are going to a

party, a baby shower for someone Eve said was called Oak. Roisin is wearing brand-new clothes which she bought especially for today.

'I am ready,' Roisin says.

'You can't wear that,' Eve responds, almost kindly. 'I'll pick something out for you.'

She finishes tying the laces with a flourish then stomps through to the living room.

Roisin rubs her burnt tongue back and forth against the backs of her teeth. She is not exactly thrilled about playing at Barbies.

Eve comes through with a long linen dress the colour of a satsuma.

'It goes with your hair,' she says.

Roisin strips out of her clothes, pulls the dress on over her head and goes through to the hall.

The Roisin in the mirror in the hallway looks back at the real Roisin with a confidence she can't recognise. With her hair properly cut she looks grungy in a way she used to aspire to as a teenager. Her cheeks have been hollowing out recently so that she doesn't wear contour like she did before. Her eyebags have been getting darker too though, but she supposes this just contributes to the grunge. When she moves she notices the feminine curve of her own waist, and it gives her a slightly nauseous feeling somewhere in her throat. She can't remember the last time she wore a dress.

JUNE

'You look good now,' Eve says. She is leaning back against the wall, texting.

'Thanks,' Roisin says.

*

Razz and Oak live in a brown terraced house in a residential bit of Edinburgh you would never bother going to unless you lived there. Eve and Roisin got lost in the maze of identical homes which wind like a snail shell round and round each other.

Eve leads the way – Google Maps held out in front of her like a beacon – and when they finally find the right door Razz lets them in with a clap on the back.

He shows them through the house with pride, waving to a couple of people on the way through. Eve is smiling and waving at people too, although she gets a less enthusiastic response than Razz does. This makes sense: she is not the one having the baby.

'Claire!' Eve cries.

Claire is stepping through the sliding doors which lead out to the garden.

She is wearing the same dress as Roisin but in a dark red. She does not look grungy; she looks as though she has just walked out of a photoshoot. This makes Roisin feel a bit sick.

Eve flings her arms around her tightly. Claire stands

stiffly and doesn't look at Roisin.

'Oh my god. It's so funny that you're wearing that dress because look at what Roisin is wearing! I picked it out for her. Honestly, she's useless at that sort of thing. But you look gorgeous, I love your earrings, are they coral? Stunning.'

Eve reaches out to touch them, and Claire shifts back on her feet slightly so that Eve's hand grasps at thin air instead. Eve laughs to cover up the moment, and Claire walks off without saying anything.

Eve grabs Roisin's hand and pulls her lightly over to the kitchen, towards the alcohol and the large pile of presents on the kitchen table. Roisin bought Oak a soft little teddy bear with a knitted jumper on. Eve said that she is a keen gardener, so they also bought her some daffodil bulbs from the botanical gardens. They should come in around the time that the baby can see colour, Eve says.

Eve always chooses good gifts. For Roisin's birthday last year she gave her a teensy wee bottle of orange blossom perfume and a guidebook to walks in and around Edinburgh.

'We should go up Arthur's Seat at some point,' Roisin says to Eve.

'Yeah definitely,' she says, pouring them both two large gins in a frantic manner. 'Do you think Claire is pissed off with me?'

Claire is standing on the other side of the room in animated conversation with a very beautiful woman with a septum piercing. Eve watches Claire intently as Claire reaches out and brushes the woman's shoulder with the tips of her tattooed fingers, then draws her closer to repeat something that is very funny, apparently. Roisin wonders whether or not she should be jealous.

Roisin shrugs, which doesn't seem to comfort Eve, but the rational moment to be stressed about the interaction has passed, and Roisin can tell that Eve doesn't want her to know how flustered she is.

Eve passes Roisin her drink, and they clink and say *slàinte* even though neither of them is from the West Coast. Roisin drinks it quickly and starts to feel better about not knowing anyone.

Eve pours them each another drink and grabs Roisin's hand, dragging her out into the garden, where her boyfriend is sitting on a wooden bench. The garden is lovely, bigger than the house would suggest, and it's been draped in prayer flags and fairy lights. There is a winding path lined with tall orange flowers and though it's been a hot day, the evening air blows a gentle breeze over the tops of the trees, warning that it's about to be Baltic.

Roisin spends most of the night sitting on the wooden bench watching people get high. The wind's promise comes true quickly, and she wanders inside to grab a blanket off the sofa.

On her way back out to the garden, she pauses and goes to get herself a glass of water. The window above the kitchen sink looks out onto the garden. As Roisin runs the tap, she watches Eve, who is sitting cross-legged in the middle of the grass with her boyfriend. He is telling her a story, and she is drinking methodically, staring at Razz and Oak, who are dancing together slowly to music Roisin can't hear.

Eve's boyfriend laughs and looks at her expectantly, but Eve hasn't noticed and instead continues to watch the two dancers with an expression of unusual peace on her pale face. She looks even more beautiful than usual.

There is a light touch on the small of Roisin's back, and she shivers.

Claire moves closer, and Roisin keeps her gaze fixed on Eve, whose upturned face seems to be glowing.

Before Claire leaves to go out into the garden, she kisses Roisin on the neck. Roisin wishes she hadn't: anyone could have seen. She's starting to realise the significance of not telling Eve.

She tries to remind herself of her old defence, that Eve didn't tell her about Mark, but it feels different now. And Roisin can understand Eve sleeping with

JUNE

Mark. He was the first person who took care of her. Roisin couldn't back then, she couldn't even take care of herself. She had to watch as Eve dissolved like a paper lantern in the rain.

Claire, Roisin supposes, takes care of her. But it doesn't feel like care, it feels more like almost everything good about Roisin's life rests on Claire having access to her.

When Roisin goes back into the garden, the blanket wrapped around her like a cape, the night air hits her sharply in the face. She sits down next to Eve on the damp, cool grass and passes her the wine. Eve drinks it from the bottle in long gulps.

The wind has shifted, and the air smells strongly of hops. Roisin can tell that Eve is drunk because her head is flopping back on her neck like she's jolting awake on a plane. Her boyfriend didn't stop talking when Roisin sat down.

Roisin puts her arm around Eve, who curls into her instinctively.

He tries to finish his sentence but falls silent. Then he tells Roisin he's going to go and get his girlfriend a glass of water. He doesn't use her name.

Eve looks up at Roisin and starts to laugh.

'What?' Roisin says.

She laughs even harder and clutches at Roisin, pulling at the front of her dress to try and keep herself upright, then gives up and falls backwards, snorting. After a breath, Eve turns to her conspiratorially, still laughing, and says in a stage whisper, 'He's so fuckin boring Roisin . . .'

Roisin starts to laugh too and whispers back, 'I know.'

They collapse into giggles on the grass. Eve grabs Roisin's hand once their laughter has died down and says, 'I will leave soon, you know. I am sorry. I know I've stayed too long.'

Roisin doesn't quite know what to say to this, so she says nothing.

'I just really can't go home right now,' Eve says, pronouncing each word with drunken care, flipping onto her side to look at Roisin with an intensity Roisin rarely sees in her these days. Eve is clearly expecting her to respond, but Roisin doesn't know what to say, so she just looks right back.

Eventually Eve says, 'Don't worry. I'm working on having him invite me to live with him.' She gestures in her boyfriend's general direction, and her loose sleeve falls off her arm, exposing her pale wrist, spattered with soft blue, grey, green. But Eve moves too quickly, and the glow from the fairy lights flickers blue and green, and Roisin's head is heavy from one glass too many, and she just isn't sure.

Roisin opens her mouth to say something, but

JUNE

Eve puts her fingers roughly on Roisin's lips to stop anything escaping.

The tips of Eve's fingers tremble. Roisin can somehow feel it at the back of her throat.

'Don't worry,' she repeats. 'He'll invite me to live with him.'

Eve's eyes glimmer. Then she laughs, a sharp piercing laugh that makes the dancers turn to look at her. She falls onto her back and laughs and laughs and laughs.

Roisin falls onto her back too, landing uncomfortably on a small stone. She doesn't move, she just lets it burrow its way into her spine, imagining it boring a hole right through to her internal organs.

Eve takes a deep breath and nudges her in the side, saying teasingly, 'You and Cal can get back to your love nest soon, don't worry.'

'Aye right, he wishes,' Roisin says, nudging her back. She turns her head to the other side so that Eve can't see her face.

Claire is watching them from the entryway to the yurt, and Roisin becomes aware that she and Eve are still holding hands. Claire lifts her hand in a slight wave. Roisin pretends not to see it and shifts her gaze to look back up at the dark sky.

Eve smells like red wine and the sweet, cheap perfume she's been buying since she was fourteen. Roisin closes her eyes, grips her clammy hand tight and breathes her in.

*

Claire and Roisin are in Claire's bed, red sheets pulled up to their chins.

The aftermath is always uncomfortable. Roisin doesn't know how long it will take until it isn't. Probably until Claire stops paying her. At which point Roisin will most likely lose interest so there won't be an aftermath anyway.

Today was the first time Roisin has seen her since the party.

She caught Roisin just before she and Eve left, when Roisin was on her way to the bathroom. She followed Roisin in before she could lock the door and pressed her up against the wall, and honestly it was pretty horrible: the bathroom was covered in pee and clumps of loo roll, and Roisin kept thinking the whole time about that scene in *The L Word* with Marina and Jenny and how that was so much hotter than this. And wondering whether Claire had also seen *The L Word* or whether she was too uptight to watch something so trashy. And then Roisin started thinking about the shitty Scottish version *Lip Service*. It was definitely more of a *Lip Service* kiss.

JUNE

Roisin was deliberately cold with Claire this morning. After she declined Claire's offer of coffee and said that she had a lot to do Claire had followed her up the stairs and invited her to stay in her husband's flat in Paris.

Roisin had said maybe, that actually she had promised that she would go to the West Coast with Eve, and Claire had looked a little stunned at being turned down. It made Roisin realise that she hadn't actually ever said no to Claire. Then it made Roisin wonder whether or not she'd ever actually said yes to Claire. Thankfully, before she could think about it properly, Claire said that Eve could come too.

This is what Roisin is contemplating now, as the warm afternoon light spills over the white sheets. She's not the sort to turn down anything if it's free, but she should feel bad for using Claire so blatantly. She doesn't though, not really.

She knows that Claire has a yoga retreat booked on the 15th of July. Maybe she and Eve could go then, alone.

'So,' Roisin says, 'it's your husband's flat?'

Claire nods but doesn't elaborate, which annoys Roisin. She is very beautiful, her curls are soft and shiny, and her cheekbones sit high upon her face, but the more time Roisin spends with her the less intimidated by her she becomes so her appeal is slowly rubbing right down to the bone of Roisin's attraction: Roisin has her and Eve doesn't. Claire chose her, not Eve.

Roisin is not sure that this is quite enough for love and prosperity. But Claire's married and is her boss, and Roisin sleeps curled up with shit she stole from her best friend, so love and prosperity was never really on the cards.

'I'm free the week of the 15th,' Roisin says.

Claire moves closer, wrapping her arms around Roisin's waist and kissing her shoulder blades. The kiss feels like an itch and makes Roisin cringe. She is hit with a strong urge to run.

'Thank you,' Claire says. 'I'll book the flights.'

FOUR: JULY

ROISIN AND EVE ARE sitting licking the sticky icing from Krispy Kreme doughnuts from their fingers and being served free tea and coffee somewhere over the Channel.

Claire realised she had booked the yoga retreat after she booked the flights, so for a small surcharge she changed her name to Eve's. Roisin knows she has fucked her way to a free holiday, which is not something she is proud of exactly, but she thinks that if anyone deserves a holiday, it's her. This is not necessarily true, but it makes Roisin feel better to think it.

Roisin had to ask Claire to ask Eve herself, so that it would look like Claire had invited Eve then Roisin, not Roisin then Eve. Claire is going to fly to meet them at the end of the week, after her retreat is over.

Cal's initial annoyance that they'd conned their way into a free holiday and hadn't invited him waned significantly once he realised that he'd have the whole flat to himself for the first time in years. He told Roisin he was going to throw an empty, but Roisin's fairly certain she's his only pal, so she's not too worried about that. She is worried he'll finish off Eve's plants though. Eve told him that he's to water them every day and left him very specific instructions, but honestly they've been getting browner and more decrepit all summer without Cal's help.

When they land in Paris the heat is like a wall. Roisin has never thought of Paris as a hot place, but she forgets how far north they are in Scotland. Getting off the plane is like stepping into a sauna.

Roisin was particularly worried going through security on the way here because if they unpacked her bag they would find the t-shirt and the anklet. For some reason she couldn't leave them at home. It felt like if she did she would lose Eve, like their connection only gets stronger the more pieces of her Roisin has, and if she leaves them behind now then Eve will run off and find some rich French boy and Roisin will never see her again.

They take the RER to Gare du Nord and wind their way through crowds of commuters, tourists, people selling fruit and vegetables underground in the labyrinthine station – to get the metro back up into the north of the city, where Claire's husband's flat is. They end up in the McDonald's in Porte de

JULY

Clignancourt, on a hot and dusty road lined with men selling cigarettes. The McDonald's is horrible: hot and loud and full of French-speakers who are justifiably unimpressed with Roisin and Eve's Standard Grade *salut un iced tea et un frites s'il vous plaît*.

But eventually they get their chips and their iced tea, and Eve pays for it, and they go outside into the baking heat and lean against the wall of the McDonald's, and Eve rolls them both cigarettes even though Roisin doesn't smoke. *(You're in Paris!)*

The nicotine makes her feel dizzy in a good way, and she's happy to just follow Eve as she drags her confidently along the road to a shockingly cool bar.

Inside it is filled with a warm yellow light and lots of people drinking pints of the bar's own brew or short glasses of wine. Eve drags her towards the tables at the end of the bar as though she's been coming here all her life. The windows look out onto overgrown railway tracks, and she tells Roisin to wait where she is while she gets them drinks.

As she moves away, leaving Roisin with the rucksacks, her loose linen trousers get pulled up by the chair leg and Roisin spots a flash of silver on her ankle.

Trying not to panic, Roisin opens her rucksack and starts rifling through it. Fuck. What if Eve found it in her bag when she went to the loo? How will she explain this to her? She could say that she'd bought her a replacement to cheer her up and that it was supposed to be a surprise and *how could you go through my bag anyway that is such an invasion of privacy you bitch*.

Roisin finds the anklet nestled in the pocket of her bag with the t-shirt and breathes slowly to try to calm herself down. Eve must have bought herself a new one to replace it. Eve would never go through Roisin's things.

Eve left the front pocket of her bag open when she took her wallet. Inside is her set of keys, a lipstick, a small watermelon-scented hand sanitizer and a short brown leather notebook. Glancing up quickly, Roisin makes sure she's still at the bar, and then she slips the small brown notebook out of Eve's bag and into her own.

There is a disco ball on the ceiling rotating slowly to the sounds of people. Everyone here seems to be looking at her. The disco ball seems to Roisin to be reflecting her guilty face onto every wall, every crevice.

A man with a moustache and a Freddy Mercury tank top sits down at their table without being asked and says '*Bonsoir,*' and then lets loose a rapid smattering of French that Roisin does not understand whatsoever.

'*Je ne parle pas français,*' she says to him, in her best French accent.

JULY

'Oh right, hi,' he says, in a thick Scouse accent which takes Roisin by surprise.

'I'm waiting for my friend,' Roisin says.

He leans a little too close to her and grins. His moustache stretches so that Roisin can see the bald patches on his upper lip. 'Ahhh your *friend* . . . alright, cool, yeah, no worries. Let me buy you guys a drink.'

At this he stands up and totters away from Roisin to the bar, and she swiftly picks up both of their bags and moves to a different table.

She has a better view of Eve from here. She can see her flirting with the bartender. Roisin wonders if she's speaking English or trying out her terrible French. Maybe she'll sleep with him.

Roisin reaches into her bag and rubs the anklet between her fingertips. It's soothing.

Eve picks up the two glasses of wine and makes her way back to the table they were at before. Roisin watches as she stops in confusion. Eve's head scans quickly around the bar in a panic until Roisin calls her name and she turns, relief painted clearly on her face.

'What the fuck?' Eve says, sitting down.

Roisin explains to her about the guy with the moustache and the lesbian fetish, and Eve relaxes a bit, clearly deciding not to be annoyed.

She has brought red wine, which Roisin doesn't really like, but she has paid for it herself which is sweet, Roisin supposes. Or maybe it's just that Roisin is finding it harder and harder to be pissed off by the things that used to piss her off.

At the beginning, Roisin was worried that sleeping with Claire would drive her and Eve apart. But actually, having something she knows Eve wants and can't have has somehow softened the edges of Eve's personality for her.

They smile at each other and sip their wine and try not to make eye contact.

It feels like being on a first date. It could be the tiredness from the travel or the nicotine or the alcohol or the sick feeling Roisin has from eating but there is a palpable atmosphere between them.

'I can't believe we've like, never gone on holiday together before,' Eve says.

Roisin nods in agreement even though she can believe it. Eve has never stayed still long enough for them to plan anything. She gets moods where she is fairly level, if her usual, mercurial self. And then suddenly without warning, everything flips and you can see that grain of fear behind her eyes that it is all going to get too mundane again, that she won't be able to bear it and she'll feel the need to fling herself off a cliff and dissolve like salt in the deep grey sea.

But Roisin won't think about that tonight. Tonight all she wants to think about is the fact that she is in

JULY

Paris, that she didn't have to buy her own drink, and that for one whole week she gets to be with Eve every single day.

Roisin can see the bartender watching Eve. She doesn't know how Eve does it, but even though she's grotty from the plane and Roisin can see stains slowly melting under her arms from the heat of the bar, Eve has captured everyone's attention. Roisin could be imagining it, but she thinks that everyone here wants her. It makes Roisin feel special that out of all the people in Paris, she is the one who gets to talk to her.

Eve starts going on about her boyfriend, which makes Roisin really notice how unbearably stuffy it is in the bar. She feels grateful for the wine and drinks it too quickly. Roisin's hair is beginning to stick to the back of her neck, and her eyes feel dry from the recycled air on the plane.

'He's a nice guy, he's just like, dull. The only good bit is that I don't actually have to sleep with him.'

Roisin doesn't think that he's a nice guy. She wants to ask her why she's still with him, but she knows why she's still with him. Roisin knows the euros in her purse didn't come from a job, or her parents. Roisin sort of likes that Eve is at least clearly using him. But Roisin wishes she wasn't so reliant upon him.

She knows too that Eve is using her and Cal, if only for their flat. Roisin doesn't really mind this either.

Roisin used Eve for her money for long enough that they're probably even. And if Eve stops using her she won't be with her any longer, and that would be worse.

Roisin gets a text: Claire wants to know if they landed safely and got to the flat okay. Roisin ignores it; she'll reply to her when they get in. Roisin doesn't know why she is behaving this way toward Claire, but she thinks it might just be because she can. Maybe Claire wants her because Roisin clearly doesn't want her in return. It could explain why Claire doesn't want Eve, because Eve wants Claire so badly. Maybe, Roisin thinks, it's why Eve doesn't want her. Roisin's thoughts have become so jumbled she closes her eyes tight for a second to recalibrate. When she opens them again Eve is looking at her intently.

'Really, you know, he treats me so well,' Eve says, smiling without her eyes. 'He's asked me to move in with him.'

The noise from the bar seems to dim a little. Roisin knew this is what Eve had planned but didn't think she would manage to pull it off quite so soon.

Roisin asks Eve what she said to him, and she replies that she's told him she'll consider it because they haven't been together very long. But, Eve says, she's going to say yes. When Eve tells Roisin this she looks at her expectantly, but Roisin doesn't say anything because she doesn't know what to say. Roisin wants to tell Eve she'll take care of her, but she can't. Roisin can't give her what she needs – her primary source of income is reliant upon sleeping with the woman she knows Eve wants.

So a man, a real man with a house and a car and an effortless income flowing in from a city so far south of the border it's a whole different world – he can give her security and friends and a life away from the half-life she's been sustaining with a family who have grown to hate her or one where she sleeps on Roisin's sofa and argues with Cal. It's an opportunity even if it's also a trap.

'What do you think?' Eve says.

Roisin knows that there is a right thing to say here, that there is a protocol to follow, magic words that break the spell that these men weave, in and around their women. But Roisin doesn't know what they are.

She thought it would be something she learned when she grew up. But now she's supposed to be grown-up, and the girls and the women never stop turning to her, asking her to say the magic words, and Roisin still doesn't know what they are. All she's learned to do is to try to ignore it as much as you can because if you're wrong, or if you kick up too much of a fuss, they stop talking to you completely. Roisin can't let that happen with Eve.

Roisin wants to tell her that she shouldn't do it, tell

her that there is another way out, but she can't. She'd be a liar and a hypocrite because she thinks that if Claire offered all that to her she would take it too.

Whether Eve likes him or not is neither here nor there, and Roisin knows in this moment as Eve looks at her with bright eyes and sweat-slicked hair in an unfamiliar bar in an unfamiliar city that she will continue having this same conversation for the rest of her life.

*

When they get to the flat – close enough to Montmartre to be bougie, far away enough to be edgy and up-and-coming – they both crash into bed without undressing or even turning on the lights. The wine has gone to their heads, and the room whirls, spinning as though it has its own gravitational pull.

There are two rooms, two double beds, but they sleep in the same one, curled up like commas. They face away from each other in exactly the same position only mirrored, like someone has taken a photograph of one of them and flipped it.

*

JULY

The next day Roisin rises early. The sun is filtering through the blinds, and she wakes up with a cool light behind her eyes. She pads through to the living room, trying not to wake Eve.

Roisin didn't get a chance to look at the place properly when they arrived in the dark, but it is beautiful, obviously. The floors are polished parquet, and like in Claire's Edinburgh flat, every object has been selected with deliberation and care. Most things are soft white or made from a burnt orange wood. Dotted around the flat are trinkets (sorry, *objets d'art*) in shades of red and orange.

When Roisin opens the fridge it is empty save for a very beautiful bottle of wine and a jar of artisanal apricots in honey. Neither looks like something someone could consume. Instead, they seem to be owned for their beauty. Roisin is starving. It's unusual for her to notice that these days. She's been hungry less and less frequently recently; ever since she had to nick food off Cal, eating has felt like more and more like a luxury that her body has decided she doesn't deserve. But the doughnuts and the chips she ate yesterday seem to have kickstarted her stomach. It aches; Roisin feels empty and sick.

She is still in her clothes from last night. She grabs the keys and her phone from the kitchen table, and rummages in her bag for her purse. It is nestled at the bottom next to the little brown book she stole from Eve's bag yesterday so she grabs both of them and shoves them quickly into her tote bag.

She pulls on her trainers and heads downstairs, out into the city. It's going to be another hot day, she can tell. It's not yet 9 o'clock, and the sun is beating down onto the pavement. She stops to lean against the wall of a building and Googles *boulangerie near me*. There is one on the corner of the street, which she heads towards.

Roisin didn't bring sunglasses, and she has to narrow her eyes and shield them with her hand as she walks down the hill. She's been to Paris once before, but she doesn't know this area at all. It's quiet, a Saturday morning; only a couple of people are on the street, walking slowly home cradling warm bread.

It is not like Edinburgh here. Roisin feels as though there's a coating of her city on her and the Parisians can tell from a mile off that she's foreign. She catches a glimpse of herself in a shop window. She has a tiny, spiky braid in her fringe and she is wearing mismatched jewellery from charity shops. Although she is out of place here in Paris, in Edinburgh she has dissolved what remained of herself from before this summer in order to blend in with her new family. She looks like Eve, she thinks, but worse.

She reaches the boulangerie, getting there just in time as a queue forms rapidly behind her. She orders

JULY

a baguette, two cafés crèmes and two pains au chocolat in halting French. The woman behind the counter is brisk and efficient despite the hordes of wasps buzzing around her head and crawling over her hands. She bats them gently from the pastries in an annoyed manner, like a schoolteacher waving away an irritating question. Roisin hands over ten euros, and the woman spits the change back and, with a staccato remark, sends her out of the door.

Roisin drinks the coffee on the walk home, sipping gingerly amid the hot steam. It's too strong for her tastes, but she needs to wake up. The smell of the warm bread mingles with the scent of the morning: wood and hot skin. Roisin sits down on the steps of a café which has not yet opened and tears chunks from the baguette ravenously until it is all gone.

She sits for a moment, just breathing. The streets are very quiet; there is nobody to see her here. All the shutters are closed. There is only a young woman in flip-flops walking her dog along the other side of the road. She is wearing joggers and a matching sweatshirt, and Roisin has no clue how she isn't dripping with sweat.

Roisin reaches into her bag and pulls out the little brown notebook. On the front page is written *Eve – Paris* in Eve's scrawled handwriting. On the second page Eve has noted the dates and times of the flights, the address of the Paris flat, and nothing else.

Roisin rifles through the notebook furiously. There is nothing at all. Not a single word. On the back of the book is a WHSmith £4.99 sticker. Eve must have bought it in the airport while Roisin went to get the doughnuts.

Roisin feels sick. What was the point of stealing it? Why couldn't there be something inside that would make it worth her while? Why hadn't Eve bothered to make it worth her while? There is a rising feeling of something awful crawling up the inside of her chest and a rancid stench coming from the drain to her right.

Roisin throws up all of the bread. Her eyes stream, and her chest aches, and she feels far too hot, and there's sweat building up at the back of her neck. She can't seem to stop retching. Even well after there is nothing else left to throw up, bile keeps billowing out of her mouth and pooling at her feet.

Once it's over, she takes some deep breaths until she starts feeling more normal, if a bit wobbly. The woman walking her dog is staring at her. Roisin stares back at her hard until she hurries her dog down the street and away from her.

Roisin puts the small brown notebook and the paper bag which held the baguette in the nearest bin and walks back to the flat slowly. When she returns, Eve comes through to the living room. She looks

JULY

beautiful in an effortless way, as though she's off to brunch. Roisin wonders if Eve worried about her when she was gone.

Wordlessly, Eve takes her coffee and pours it into a mug from the cupboard. She opens the bag of pastries and sits down on the cream-coloured sofa with a sigh.

'Thanks,' she says.

Roisin shrugs and tells her she was too hungry to wait and not to worry about it. She takes her takeaway cup and goes to sit on the sofa too. The smell is too strong and Roisin has to hold it away from herself, trying to breathe through her mouth.

As Eve eats the pastry she drops flakes of it onto the sofa. She takes a sip of coffee and a bit dribbles out of the lip of the mug and plops onto the cream fabric. She has made her mark here already.

Roisin asks her how she slept, and Eve says fine and then tells her she wants to go and get all of the touristy shite out of the way today so that for the rest of the week they can do Paris the proper way. Roisin nods her head in agreement but wonders what it is exactly Eve knows about *doing* Paris.

Eve wipes the last crumbs from her lips and stretches like a cat, saying she's going to go for a shower. Then she looks at Roisin, really looks at her for the first time this morning, and Roisin shrinks a little under her gaze. Eve scans her oily brow and the crust of sleep on her eyes and the V-shaped sweat mark down the front of her t-shirt.

'You look nice,' she says, and Roisin hopes Eve can't smell the vomit on her breath as she replies: 'Thanks.'

*

The touristy stuff that Eve wanted to do ended up taking up a good part of the week. She wanted to see the Louvre, the Musée d'Orsay, the Picasso Museum, the Arc de Triomphe, the Tuileries, the Eiffel Tower; she wanted to eat at Les Deux Magots and Café de Flore and get macarons from Ladurée. Eve shells out crisp banknotes like she would Monopoly money.

They arrived on the Friday; it is now Wednesday, and today they have both agreed to go to Père Lachaise to see the grave of Oscar Wilde. They decide to leave early to make the most of the day but end up catching the commuter rush, spending half an hour crushed against the doors by tight-lipped Parisians who smell like cigarettes, sharp, sticky sweat and expensive perfume. They clamber out of the humid metro onto a bustling road, and Eve proclaims immediately that she is just dying for a coffee so they sit outside and order a café crème each and a croissant to share, which Eve eats.

Food spills from every corner of Paris. People walk down the streets tearing the tops off their baguettes,

JULY

tourists eat crêpes and macarons on benches in the parks. There is a café and a boulangerie on each street, a veg shop, a mini supermarket, a man selling chestnuts from a hot grate. This overwhelming scent mingles with the thick, rotten heat of the city, and Roisin just can't touch any of it.

Eve drinks her coffee slowly, dunking the ends of the croissant into it. She has blended right into the city. Her clothes look expensive in the right way, and she has modified the way she does her makeup so that it is lighter and fresher, more suited to French tastes.

'So where is his grave exactly then?' Eve says.

Roisin shrugs and pulls out her phone. There is something surreal about typing *oscar wilde grave* into Google Maps. Even weirder is that it works: the algorithm has plotted out a quick and easy route directly through the lush green death, and it's not too far from where they're sitting.

Eve scrapes the last dregs of foam out of her cup with a teaspoon and surveys the busy street. 'Shall we go then?'

Roisin abandons her coffee and follows her through the gates.

The cool shelter of the trees is a welcome relief from the heat. They both slow down to take sips of water from a crumpled plastic bottle with condensation forming on the inside. Eve strides out in front confidently, even though Roisin is the one who knows where to go.

Roisin doesn't believe in ghosts, but there is the sort of presence in the graveyard that you feel when you walk into a church. She feels chilled, weighted down by it. She breathes in and almost expects to smell frankincense and cheap wax. She can't remember the last time she set foot in a church. It was probably with Eve, when they were younger.

Eve reaches a crossroads and hesitates. Roisin checks her phone and calls out 'Left!', and Eve marches on as though it had been her intention all along.

They walk in silence the rest of the way; Roisin only catches up with her when they have to turn down a dusty side path.

Oscar Wilde's grave is immediately evident because it is caged within glass. There is a sign in French and English taped to it which asks people not to leave any marks. This has not worked: it is covered in lipstick prints in a hundred shades of pink and red, everyone trying to leave their mark, their love, the biggest print, the brightest shade, the most important.

Eve whips out a red lipstick and paints her lips carefully using the reflection from her phone like a mirror, then kisses the glass. She passes the lipstick to Roisin, who does the same, right next to hers. As if kissing Eve by proxy.

Eve starts to say something, then stops.

JULY

'What?' Roisin asks.

Eve shrugs and hesitates a moment before she says, 'I hope people like me this much when I die.'

Roisin knows that everyone dies, in the end, but as Eve says the word *when* the concreteness of it thuds against her chest. Roisin leans her head on Eve's shoulder, ostensibly to comfort her, but really because Roisin is worried she might pass out. Roisin can see Eve's breath, feel her heart pounding through her neck.

Eve reaches out to smudge the lipstick artfully so that their two prints are connected. She entwines her hand with Roisin's and asks if they can go to see Notre Dame again – she wants a better picture for her Instagram.

*

That night in bed they hold each other.

They went to a bar down the road and split a bottle of white wine and flirted with a man who they had to hide from in a bathroom stall. They helped each other balance precariously on the toilet seat so he would only see one pair of feet and when he threw his whole weight against the door of the stall they tried not to laugh, a nervous laugh that threatened to spill from their mouths without their consent. They held hands and breathed in tandem, short stolen breaths, until he slammed the bathroom door behind him and yelled, *PUTES*.

They held there for another fifteen minutes, just in case. Then they ran home together, really laughing now, as though it was all one huge adventure, so funny, did you see his big blue vein on his forehead wasn't it hilarious how angry he got bet he's got a small dick what a creep oh my god.

It's only when they get home that the tears begin, full rattling sobs which seem to shake the ground. And they get into bed and turn the lights off and they rock together so that they are floating on the waves, out to sea.

*

They meet Claire the next morning, outside Gare du Nord. She is wearing her usual clothes but does not look out of place. Eve was flustered by Claire's arrival; she spent two hours getting ready this morning, and she hasn't eaten at all. Roisin was nervous too, about seeing Claire. Roisin and Eve haven't spoken about last night. In fact they barely said two words to each other. Instead they wove around each other in a dance, Eve doing Roisin's hair, Roisin picking out Eve's shoes. It was like they were both getting ready for a date.

JULY

Eve embraces Claire warmly and flutters around her, offering to carry her bag and saying thank you so much for letting them stay. Roisin doesn't say much, letting Eve babble about the flat. She lets Claire's hand linger on the small of her back when she greets her.

Claire tells them she knows a great place nearby, and they walk a short distance to a very chic-looking restaurant which is out of place among the crêpe and kebab shops. Claire and Roisin sit on a bench against the wall, facing Eve. Roisin and Eve order the exact same thing as Claire does just in case she pays, and they all sit and look at each other and smile, and Roisin tries to think of something, anything, to say.

'So how are you finding the flat?' Claire asks, even though they covered this on the walk over.

They both nod enthusiastically, and Eve launches again into her spiel about the area and the great little coffee place they found and how beautiful the flat is. As she talks, Claire slides her hand along the bench, under the table, until it is resting on Roisin's thigh. Roisin hopes Eve can't see. Her hand is cool against Roisin's warm skin, and it feels nice to be wanted, to be touched so deliberately.

Eve falls silent, having exhausted the topic, then after a moment she addresses Claire again, saying, 'I bought a replacement, by the way, for the anklet you gave me.'

At this, Claire sits up a little straighter. Eve sticks out

her leg to show her, and Claire says that it is very nice. They are looking at each other intently.

Roisin has brought the original anklet with her. It comforted her to have it on the walk over here, rubbing it between her fingers as they marched in silence towards the station. Now, though, it brands her, burning through the pocket of her shorts. Claire's hand is inching closer to it, further up her leg.

Roisin excuses herself to go to the toilet. She splashes cold water on face and considers flushing the anklet down the toilet. After thinking for a moment, she comes to the conclusion that she couldn't do that without having a panic attack so instead she takes off one of her trainers and stuffs the anklet into her sock, right down at the bottom so that it lies flat against the top of her foot. She puts her trainer back on and goes back to the table. She sits down, and Claire puts her hand back on her thigh, right where it was before.

'We were just saying,' Claire says, 'it'd be nice to go and get some wine and maybe a baguette and sit in a park this afternoon? I'd love to hear what you guys have been up to.'

Eve nods. Roisin says that sounds good, and their waiter brings them three identical salads with three identical drinks, and they eat steadily in silence. Claire pays.

JULY

★

That night Eve and Roisin sleep in separate rooms. Claire insisted that she sleep on the sofa so that they could get a bed each, and neither of them protested, which was lucky because Roisin didn't want her to know they'd been sleeping in the same bed.

Roisin can't sleep without the warm weight of Eve beside her and finds herself tossing and turning, getting hotter and hotter until she starts seeing things moving in the corners of the room and has to get up for a glass of water.

Claire is still awake. She is sitting fully clothed on the sofa with a mug beside her, reading something in French. She looks up when Roisin comes through and smiles at her, as though she'd expected her to do so all along.

Roisin gets a glass of water and drinks it steadily next to the sink. She feels as though she has walked out onto a chessboard by mistake.

Roisin goes through to the bathroom without making eye contact with Claire. Her head is a bit fuzzy from standing up too quickly: she trips on the little stone step which leads into the bathroom and has to catch herself against the glass of the shower door. It makes an oddly loud rattling noise. She steadies herself against it and looks blearily into the mirror over the sink. Her wide dark eyes stare back at her. The sight of her own gaunt face is unnerving so she closes her eyes and takes deep breaths.

She feels Claire come up behind her and kiss her on the back. Claire smells like coffee, and Roisin wonders if she's been drinking it to stay awake. She wonders why Claire hasn't just come through to her room, why she's waited for her. It's not as though Roisin can say no. Maybe creating an illusion of agency makes Claire feel better about everything.

When Roisin opens her eyes it is not her own face she sees reflected in the mirror but Eve's.

She is standing behind them, mouth slightly open, eyes heavy with sleep, a terrible expression of grief on her face. Claire hasn't noticed, she is still kissing Roisin, and now her fingers are inside her, and Roisin can't say anything, it's as if someone has plastered over her mouth so that she can't talk anymore, and she can only watch as Eve's face contorts into a silent laugh. She is laughing at Roisin, laughing at Claire, laughing at the vulgarity of it all. Eve turns and walks away, out of the front door and into the night alone.

And then Claire touches her again and Roisin tries not to think too hard about it.

FIVE: AUGUST

THE HEATWAVE HAS HIT its peak in Edinburgh. It's got to the point where everyone is tired of it. The first few days saw the majority of the city skive off work to go and get smashed in a park, any park. But now men pause on short walks to the wee Tescos to rest their sweating bodies languidly against trees or the corners of buildings and young children, red-faced and sticky, walk their bikes in the shaded part of the street.

Cal and Roisin have been keeping the blinds pulled down all day in order to keep the heat out. It's meant that her healthy Parisian glow has vanished, and they've both ended up with the drawn, pallid faces of Austen invalids.

Eve did not return to the flat after she found Roisin and Claire together. Roisin didn't tell Claire that Eve had seen them.

Afterwards, Claire went back to the sofa, and Roisin went back to her bed and stayed up all night, cross-legged at the top of the mattress, waiting for the click of the front door. But she knew Eve wouldn't come back. Eve does not do things by halves.

In the morning she let Claire discover Eve's absence, staying silent through her fluttering and panic.

'It's fine,' she told her finally, when it became too much to bear. 'She used to do this all the time. Honestly, she'll be back home.'

Sure enough, her passport, wallet and keys had been picked up from the living-room table.

Roisin had to carry all Eve's things, lugging two heavy backpackers' rucksacks on the RER through to Roissy, and pay to take the extra bag on the flight. She left before Claire, who wanted some time to *decompress*. The journey back was a lonely, sweaty struggle. At one point, as the train reached Saint-Denis, Roisin considered ditching both of their bags and getting out of the carriage, starting a new life in a new place with new sights and sounds where she could speak new words in a new language that she had never spoken for Eve. But this was too much of a decision for Roisin to make, and she stayed on the train instead. Even though staying on the train was also a decision, it did not involve disrupting the flow of life in any way, and therefore felt like less of one.

The living room feels strange to her now. Even though nothing has changed, not really, it echoes;

AUGUST

it never used to echo. The sofa is still dented heavily from Eve's body. Roisin can't decide if it is more or less comfortable now.

She can't remember how she and Cal used to live. They're still watching *Love Island* at the kitchen table instead of the living room. This is partially because they haven't bothered to link the telly back up but also because it still feels to Roisin too much like trespassing on Eve's space to go in there. Roisin feels as though Eve has died and they've built a memorial to her. Her things are still just as they were when she was living in the flat. Roisin hasn't unpacked Eve's stuff from Paris, she just left it all in a bag behind the sofa.

Cal hasn't asked why Eve left. Roisin thinks he knows by now when to leave her alone. He hasn't even mentioned her name. So it's a surprise to her when he suggests Roisin move into the living room.

'Here though, listen, if Eve's not coming back it makes sense. It's got way more room, and we never use it anyway. We could push her stuff into the corner and buy an actual bed frame, shove one of the sofas against the back wall in the kitchen. You could keep one in your room if you wanted. Cause a was thinking then maybe a could have the box room as an office?'

They are sitting at the kitchen table with the blinds drawn, watching *Love Island*. Cal gave her a run-down when she got back from Paris about all the drama and recouplings she'd missed. There's an ad break at the moment so he's making another cup of tea.

She hasn't ever really thought about it. It's probably good to change up the living room a bit, though, make it more liveable again. And there's something quite nice, she thinks, about sleeping where Eve used to sleep. Roisin's been struggling to drift off since she got home – curled up with the anklet, she is on and off her phone or up and down the ladder most of the night to get water.

She hasn't been to work since Paris. Claire hasn't pulled her up on it yet. Honestly, Roisin's been feeling really weird about the whole thing since they got back. Last night she scrolled through Indeed looking for jobs, but it became depressing very quickly. She has realised that she is not qualified for anything other than café work. Her degree is pretty much useless unless it's accompanied by at least three months of an internship, which she either couldn't, or simply didn't, do.

There is a café down the road which is hiring, but Roisin isn't sure she'd get a reference from her old boss, and even if she did, would she be able to face going back to shift work? She briefly considered signing up for Universal Credit but remembered a friend doing that a year or so ago and ending up with £20 a week in exchange for being routinely humiliated. Surely at this point in her life she deserves something more. Surely the world owes her something more than that.

Of course, she is beginning to understand that it doesn't. The world doesn't owe anyone anything, especially not money. That's the whole point. That's why Eve has chosen her boyfriend, and it's why Roisin slipped into Claire's pocket for a taste of comfort and freedom, just for a moment.

'Yeah alright,' Roisin says. 'As long as I don't have to pay extra in rent?'

Cal shakes his head. 'Nah, don't worry about it.'

Roisin moves into the living room the next day. They get a free bedframe off Gumtree, dropped off that morning in parts, and Roisin nearly breaks her ankle getting the mattress down from her old bed. She and Cal get the bus to IKEA and buy new sheets and a bedside table (he pays) and sit and eat Daim cake and drink tea (Roisin pays) looking out onto the carpark and the Pentland Hills beyond it. For a moment Roisin thinks that there is snow on the hills, but when she points it out to Cal he tells her it's fake: the Snowsports Centre.

On the way back they sit up at the top of the bus, right at the front so that when they spiral down the roads into the city it's as though they're on a rollercoaster. When they were wee, she and Eve used to come into the city and just sit on the bus all day, sharing headphones from an MP3 player and swapping different flavours of Hubba Bubba bubblegum. Eve would paint Roisin in thick layers of Dream Matte Mousse, and Roisin would show Eve how to backcomb her hair just so – so that she looked like a shit version of Alexa Chung. Then they'd get off at random and sit in a park for a bit and do the exact same thing, and then they'd get back on the bus and do it again. And the next weekend and the weekend after that and the weekend after that. Roisin thinks it might be *that* Eve she wants back. Or that happiness, the ability to feel like you can sit on a bus all day because you'll never run out of time in an endless summer.

At home, Cal cracks open his dusty toolbox that hasn't seen any action since they lost their corkscrew and tried to use a spanner instead. They assemble the rickety bedframe together. When they are done the room looks bare but nice. She takes a picture to text to Eve but then she doesn't. Eve hasn't contacted Roisin since Paris.

Roisin almost texts Claire, but it would be too hard to come up with an excuse for not turning up to work. Just to really sink the depression in, Roisin clicks into her banking app and looks at the dwindling figure. She's not sure how she's managed to spend all the money from Claire already but she has, so there's no point even thinking about it.

To distract herself, she logs into Facebook to stalk

AUGUST

Eve. Eve hasn't blocked her yet, but she has only posted pictures from Paris that don't have Roisin in them. An hour ago she posted a picture of herself in Kelvingrove Park.

*

The train to Glasgow is packed and sweltering and horrible. It's the Fringe, and there is an Old Firm match on so the carriage is full of Celtic supporters and hungover art-student types with bad haircuts. No doubt if Roisin had entered a different carriage, it would have been full of Rangers supporters and hungover art-student types with bad haircuts. Everyone is drinking openly, which makes Roisin feel better about drinking Lidl own-brand vodka from Eve's water bottle. You cannot buy anything that tastes more like paint stripper than Lidl own-brand vodka, but its appeal lies in its horribleness: if it weren't so horrible it would be more expensive.

When Roisin gets into Glasgow it is just as busy as Fringe-laden Edinburgh. There are police on horseback outside the station. One of the horses is pulling at the bit, mouth frothing.

Roisin doesn't really know where it is she is going. If Eve is still in Glasgow Roisin isn't sure who she would be staying with so, on a whim, she decides to head to Byres Road.

Glasgow is thick with people. Throngs of blue and green split the streets like two branches of the same rushing burn. It's hot, hotter than Roisin has ever experienced in Glasgow. The sun beats down so heavily that she sticks to the shaded side of the street, feeling the skin on her nose burning. Sauchiehall Street looks run-down. Roisin remembers hearing about some fire, somewhere along here. She can't remember if it was the art school, and if it was, she can't remember if it has burnt down once or twice. Despite this, everyone looks pretty happy. There are more goths than there are people dressed like lifestyle YouTubers.

When she reaches Charing Cross she is almost hit by a car.

This is because she ignored the red light and walked out into the road without looking because let's face it, they'll stop for her, and if they don't what's the difference.

When the driver blares his horn Roisin sticks two fingers up at him and tells him to go fuck himself. Roisin feels powerful, suddenly, and the look of fear on his face only makes her feel a wee bit ill.

The buildings in Glasgow are darker and warmer than in Edinburgh. The red brick casts a deep shadow. Slowly though, as you enter the West End, they turn the familiar pale yellow of Edinburgh. The air becomes a little lazier, the people a little more monied. Roisin passes florists, vegan bakeries, coffee shops with hand-painted signs.

Roisin orders an iced coffee and three of the same cake from a café on Great Western Road. There is a large mirror propped against the back wall on which they have written the specials. She observes herself as though she is someone else. The woman who looks back is not wearing a bra. She has not brushed her hair or her teeth. There are dark shadows under her eyes. Roisin looks harder. She actually think it makes her look kind of hot. She musses up her hair a little bit more. The barista catches her doing this and is evidently suppressing laughter when she hands Roisin the coffee and the three massive cakes. Roisin leaves without tipping her the spare change because she is trying to be frugal and also because she is a bitch. Roisin trips over a very small Jack Russell on her way out.

As Roisin continues to walk slowly up Great Western Road she takes a bite of the cake. It turns out to be mostly peanut butter and she thinks maybe dates. For some reason Roisin can't swallow it she keeps chewing and chewing until it is sticky mush swilling around her mouth. She spits it out onto the ground and puts the rest of the cakes into the bin even though they were really really expensive, but even the thought of them sitting in her bag waiting for her later makes her want to throw up.

Roisin sucks down some of the iced coffee to get the taste out of her mouth, and it is when she comes up for air that she notices a girl with short blonde hair turn down a side street towards the university.

It isn't Eve, of course. This girl's hair is darker, more natural-looking. She is too tall, and her walk isn't quite right. But Roisin follows her anyway, as though she is Alice following the white rabbit, because some part of her believes that this is a sign from God, a sign from anyone, that this girl might know who Roisin is, know what and who she needs, and that the girl might lead Roisin to her.

Roisin follows her past tall buildings lined by shady trees and up the hill and then back down again until they reach the Hillhead Bookclub, where the girl embraces a middle-aged woman who has the same short blonde hair and the same confident walk, and they go in together.

Now at a loss for what to do, Roisin sits at one of the empty tables outside of the Bookclub. There are women doing a silent disco down the road. Everyone is walking steadily past them with their eyes glued to the ground.

The year Roisin first left home, she came here to meet Eve, who was crashing with a friend. Eve met her off the train, and it rained the whole day. They walked up Great Western Road in the drizzle, and Eve bought a leather jacket from a vintage shop and a musty old French paperback from Otago Lane, and then they went to the University Café because one of Eve's friends had said it was where all the students went, but it was completely empty. They both ordered chips, cheese and curry sauce and ate it steadily in silence at a Formica table together. Then they came here and had strawberry mojitos, and then they went to the botanical gardens and watched the fog swirl around the rhododendrons. And then they both went home, their separate ways. As Roisin sat on the train, watching the Trossachs disappear behind the city, she thought about the way things used to be and that maybe things had changed too much for them to still be friends.

But then Eve came through to Edinburgh a week later and they stayed up until the sun started to rise on the winter morning, and they took a flask of tea up Calton Hill and poured it into proper mugs Roisin nicked off Cal and watched the city wake up together, huddled under the same big blanket. Sometimes, Roisin thinks, friends can only be friends in certain cities, in certain lights.

Roisin does not want to see the girl. She wants to go home. She wants to lie down on the sofa, fit her body into the shape that Eve's left and melt right down into the fabric until she becomes her, until her body becomes Eve's body, her brain becomes Eve's brain, so that she can never ever leave.

Roisin walks back the exact same way she came, past the coffee shop, over Charing Cross. Her head is heavy from the alcohol and the hot hot sun, and she can feel the ground underneath her shifting like sand dunes, the street lamps swaying in the breeze.

It is just as she is turning right where Sauchiehall Street becomes Buchanan that – like a mirage – she sees her in the distance. And him. It never crossed her mind that she would be with him. The sun is setting over them, and the soft trail from her cigarette swirls around their heads like they're both daydreaming. They probably are. They look very much in love. He leans over and kisses her gently on the top of the head, and she smiles up at him and laughs.

Roisin sits down on the hard ground and cries. Her body feels frozen, the way your cheeks freeze up after one too many drinks. She sits on the steps of the St Enoch Centre, watching a man on his soapbox scream about the devil as tears stream silently down her face, for what feels like hours. She stretches her hands open and closed, open and closed, open and closed.

The feeling begins to come back to her toes, and she tries to stand up, but the blood rushes to her head, and for a blissful moment she can't see anything at all. She starts walking back up Sauchiehall Street blindly, with no real purpose. It is only when she reaches St Aloysius that she realises where she has been headed. She flicks a stale cornflake off the hem of her jumper and steps over the threshold.

Inside the world stops, as it always does. The high, dark arches smell both musty and cool. She does not go to the main altar. Instead she slots some change into a metal stand and picks out a fresh IKEA tea light. She stares at the statue of Jesus on the cross. He looks down, away from the stained glass and the frescoes on the ceiling, towards where she stands. Roisin wishes she felt more for him than she does, but right now she can only think of Eve.

Roisin brushes the tea light against someone else's flame, watching as it licks at the wax. She blows a sheet of breath at it softly, and it swells. She places it right at the top, in the middle. The biggest flame, the brightest love, the most important.

*

Claire's house has not changed.

Of course it hasn't. It's been less than a month since Roisin was here. Why would it have changed? But it seems as though the whole world has shifted on its axis slightly so Roisin has been going through her days expecting the sky to be green.

She has not been home yet. She sat on the steps of St Aloysius until the sky turned and then, against her better judgement, she went to Best Kebab on Dundas Street.

She ordered a samosa, and they overcharged her for it, and then she couldn't eat it so she just sat on the curb outside and stared at it wishing she'd saved her money. By then it was getting very dark, and she probably should have been worried about being a woman sitting alone in an alley behind a train station, but the thing, Roisin thought, about being a teenager surrounded by dodgy people is that after making it to adulthood a kind of God complex begins to develop. If she survived that, she'll survive this. Maybe she can't die. Maybe it wouldn't be so bad if she did. Is that a God complex or is it suicidal ideation? Are they the same thing? Either way it makes being a drunk woman in a dark alley a lot less stressful.

Roisin got the second to last train back to Edinburgh in the pitch black, so that it felt as though the whole journey was in a tunnel underground, as though she would never resurface. Her reflection stared at her from the dark glass of the train window.

When Roisin arrived back in Edinburgh it was pouring with rain. Thunder cracked in the distance.

AUGUST

Maybe the heatwave was finally breaking. The rain felt pleasantly cool against her skin, licking her clean.

Roisin decided that going home to that room with that sofa with that brand new unslept-in bed would be the absolute worst thing in the entire world. So she went to McDonald's and bought a large coke and sat up the top chewing on the ice. There were a couple of homeless men sitting to her right and a couple of face-glittered Edinburgh Uni students at the end of their night out to her left. Both groups ate methodically in a bleary silence until the staff kicked them all out at closing.

After she was removed from the building, she started to wander north, away down the hill.

Roisin stopped in the middle of the road right at the top next to St Andrews Square. There was a pale light on the horizon. The city was cold and quiet and still. She could see down to the blinking lights of the Forth Road Bridge, the hills beyond.

She went on, following the light as it wound through the tall buildings, first of the New Town, then down into Stockbridge, watching lights switch on in the dark windows, watching people wake up. She really wanted a hot drink: for the first time in weeks it was properly cold, and her fingers were turning blue at the tips. There was nowhere open yet, so she made her way to Inverleith Park to wait.

She sat hunched on a bench until the early-morning joggers appeared, and then she went to go and get herself a coffee. Roisin was beginning to panic about how much money she'd spent. She definitely couldn't afford to buy things on a whim like this anymore, but being comfortable is a habit that she has yet to snap out of.

At the very moment that she exited the coffee shop, like divine retribution, a seagull shat on her. This is why Roisin is at Claire's. Not for human warmth or connection, but for a shower and a washing machine.

Roisin woke her up by banging very loudly on her front door, and then she shouted very loudly at the window for Claire to fucking let her in because a fucking seagull fucking shat on her.

Roisin thinks that Claire is probably very pissed off at her, which is making her quite pleased with herself. Her rage is not scary or intimidating. It's just a wee bit funny. She means so little to Roisin that Claire could punch her and Roisin probably wouldn't care. She'd bounce right back up like those wavy inflatable things they have outside car sales rooms in America. Over and over and over again like a bizarre, grinning punching bag.

Roisin used Claire's expensive shampoo and her expensive conditioner, and then she poured some of her expensive shower gel out onto the expensive tiles.

AUGUST

It pooled at her feet like honey, like liquid gold. With every second it spilled Roisin counted the drops: £1, £2, £3, £4.

Then Roisin put on a pair of Claire's soft linen pyjamas and curled up behind her in bed and tried to get Claire to hold her, but her hair was wet and sticky from all of Claire's oils and elixirs, and Claire slowly moved her elbow, millimetre by millimetre, so that it jutted into Roisin's chest.

If Roisin was at home right now she would be coming down from her bed to find a mug of sweet tea with a saucer placed on top to keep the heat in. Cal usually makes her one before he leaves for work. Sometimes, if he's feeling generous or he's done something to piss her off, he'll put a banana next to it. And then Roisin remembers that she doesn't have her room anymore, it's Cal's office.

Roisin is lying beside Claire, refusing to move, watching Claire's eyes stay firmly, deliberately shut as the sun grows bright outside her window and her small yellow alarm clock begins to trill.

Roisin watches her as she pretends to wake, stretching slightly. She dresses quickly in the bathroom out of Roisin's sight and then goes downstairs. Roisin follows her and sits down at the wooden kitchen table, legs wide like a man's. Claire is making coffee. She weighs out the beans and grinds them by hand. Roisin has never seen her do this before. The tea or coffee has always been ready and waiting for her downstairs. It takes her a long time to grind the beans. Roisin doesn't think she could be bothered. Maybe if she had nothing better to do.

Claire pours the coffee grounds into the bottom of the French press, and when the kettle has boiled she pours the hot water over the top of it.

She hands Roisin a mug and sets the coffee on the table and sits down and looks at her. Roisin looks at the whorls on the wooden table.

'Why did you come here?' Claire asks her, pressing the plunger on the French press down slowly. Roisin is not very sure what to say to her.

'I needed a shower,' she says. 'A bird shat on me.'

Claire takes a deep breath.

'Why haven't you been turning up to work?'

Roisin lets this hang in the air between them. Claire seems to have realised what Roisin's silence has implied, but too late. Claire busies herself with pouring them both a coffee, the steam rising in a spiral like fruit flies trapped in a glass jar.

Roisin wants to pour it over her head.

'Does your business actually exist?' Roisin asks, instead of committing assault. 'I've been fucking about making this website for months, and I haven't seen you take a single client.'

AUGUST

Claire doesn't respond, just takes a slow sip of her coffee.

'What were you paying me for? Do you even have a husband?' Roisin demands. She knows her breath is horrible; she hasn't brushed her teeth, and she smells of alcohol and sweat. Roisin leans in closer.

'He's working,' Claire says, not meeting her gaze.

'Okay, but are you still together?' Roisin asks. A speck of Roisin's saliva lands on Claire's upper lip.

'No,' Claire replies.

'Who are you with then? Why did we have to keep this secret?' Roisin lets each question tear through her. She's fucking tired of it all, of everything, and it's all Claire's fault, how fucking dare she! Eve would never have left her if it wasn't for fucking Claire!

Claire looks up at Roisin as Roisin scrapes her chair back and stands above the table. The single light casts a tall dark shadow on the back wall so that a second Roisin looms over them both, watching.

'What about Eve?' Roisin asks, even though she knows that by asking she will not have a job anymore, even though, really, she already knows the answer. 'Did you pay her too?'

Roisin waits for Claire to reply. She doesn't. She can't look at Roisin. And so Roisin leaves, barefoot into the morning.

★

Everything has always been about Eve, Roisin thinks. All the people Roisin meets are interested in her because of Eve. It is hard to remember a time when she didn't follow Eve around, doing all the things she'd already done, just slightly worse than she did them. Everything is about Eve. Everything. And for what? All that time wasted. All that love wasted. Does love do this does it does Eve do this does she what the fuck is Roisin supposed to fucking do? Roisin screams *FUCK* so loudly she hears birds flutter out of a nearby tree, and a beautiful couple holding the sticky hands of a beautiful child cross the beautiful street to avoid her.

Roisin remembers Eve's clammy little hand holding hers as they walked, pigs to the slaughter, down the red linoleum corridor to detention, she remembers the hot, beautiful nights in sweaty Cowgate clubs where time passed like popping candy, and she remembers the damp mornings in mouldy flats. She remembers a time before time could be wasted when the clock read nothing and minutes were measured by someone else and she remembers summer hours and hours and hours spent running barefoot across gritty sand and racing screaming into filthy briney Portobello waves and she remembers the summer she first tasted alcohol and she remembers Eve holding her hair back as she vomited up purple wine and first heartbreak and menthol cigarettes and she remembers holding Eve and holding Eve and holding Eve and she remembers Eve holding her hand again but this time in the bushes behind the school as the police hunted underagers and she remembers getting drunk in carparks and in closes and in pubs and in clubs and in the Meadows and by the sea and with feet dangling over cliff's edges and she remembers Eve's amber hair spinning out from her head in the deep green reservoir and she remembers Edinburgh over and over and over and over and she remembers the sun rising on mornings that had never quite been nights and she remembers the ephemeral taste of summer fruit and she remembers Claire's hands

on her

on Eve

and she wants to stop remembering and she wants to peel off her skin peel off every part of her that has ever been touched rip it right out because it's all wrong this is all wrong. This is not how things should be.

Roisin has come to the bridge over the Water of Leith. The street is empty. She pulls her leg up onto the wall and swings onto it so that she is sitting on the thin pyramid top, feet dangling into the air below.

Roisin wobbles on the smooth stone and catches herself quickly, regaining balance with a jolt. The empty space below the bridge seems to stretch endlessly below her. She can feel the water beneath pulling her down, like the moon must feel the tides. The air is crisp and clean. The leaves on the trees that line the banks are beginning to turn.

First they will burn up amber and gold and the deepest blood-red. Then they'll melt like toffee from the branches and float away downstream, leaving the trees bare and the city undressed. Roisin can see the cold morning sun glinting off the rippled stream in short bursts. A chill blows right through her. It smells like Edinburgh.

It was all too good to be true. The weather is beginning to turn.

Roisin can hear the gulls keening on the wind. It is the only sound in the deserted street. It must be the weekend. The buildings are turned silver in the morning light, the water rustles under her feet, and *Fuck*, Roisin thinks, *I'm up high*.

The river is deep. The bronze statue of the naked man is submerged up to his neck. If she jumped, at most, she'd break her legs. Nothing else.

A seagull caws triumphantly and empties his bowels all over the statue. Roisin swings her legs back onto solid ground and starts the walk home.

★

AUGUST

It takes Roisin until she is nearly at the flat to realise that along with her shoes, phone and all her clothes, she has also left behind her keys. She is hoping and praying that Cal will be in. Honestly, Roisin thinks, Claire's fucking pyjamas are probably expensive enough that Roisin could replace everything just by hawking them on Depop.

Roisin buzzes up to the flat, and Cal lets her in without asking who it is. When she gets to the door he looks startled, as though he was expecting someone else.

'Fuck . . .' He says. 'You look like shit.'

'Yeah.' Roisin replies.

'Where the fuck are your shoes?'

Roisin shrugs, and he closes the door behind her. She sits at the kitchen table with her arms crossed tight and he makes them both a cup of tea. Then they watch telly together until he says he has to go and meet a friend, but to call him if she needs him.

Roisin didn't realise he had other friends.

Roisin considers telling him that she left her phone at Claire's, but then she would have to tell him that she was at Claire's, and then she would have to tell him why.

Awkwardly, he pats her on the back and tells her she doesn't actually look that bad. Then he leaves, and Roisin is alone again.

The girl who lives across the road is smoking out of the window. Roisin goes over and waves to her. Maybe she would love her, if she knew her. The woman raises her eyebrows briefly, then stubs out her cigarette and retreats back into the darkness of her flat.

Roisin can feel all of the caffeine and hangover and sleep deprivation fizzing behind her eyes. She goes into Cal's room and wraps herself up in his dark blue duvet and falls into a deep sleep. She dreams about the reservoir, about floating in the soft water.

When she wakes the light has changed outside the room. She can hear Cal's laptop blaring studio laughter. Her eyes are thick with sleep, and her head is pounding.

And then she realises it's not her head: it's the buzzer. There's someone at the door. She hears Cal get up from the kitchen table and let them in.

Roisin knows from the rise and fall of her voice that it is Eve. She curls up in bed and pulls the blankets over her head so that she can't hear her anymore and breathes, loudly and slowly, for what feels like hours. The wood on Cal's bedframe is soft and peeling. She scratches at it, and curls come away easily, like butter. Her finger starts to bleed, she notices, but she doesn't feel any pain.

When Roisin emerges Eve is gone, and it is raining. Cal is sitting at the kitchen table with two more cups of tea. He gestures to the one with a saucer on top, offering it to her. He looks as though he's about to tell her that he and mum are getting divorced but they still love her very very much.

'Eve came past,' he says instead.

'Yeah,' Roisin says. 'I heard.'

He nods his head slowly at this.

'She took her stuff back. There actually wasn't that much. When her shit was everywhere it was as though she fuckin owned the place but nah, she had about two bags.'

Now it is Roisin's turn to nod slowly. She picks up her tea and peers round the door into Eve's room. Roisin's room. The stuff has been removed; Cal is right. On the bed, folded neatly, is Eve's t-shirt. On top, in a perfect circle, is the anklet.

The rain beats down hard against the single-glazed windows. It feels as though it is coming into the flat; the condensation drips as though the water has managed to leak through the glass into the other side.

Roisin lifts the lower pane of the sash and case right up, letting the rain bounce off the floorboards. The branch of the tree outside flops into the room, leaves trailing on the wood. When she turns around she notices that Eve has left behind both her rhododendrons. One is much more dead than the other.

Roisin goes back into the kitchen and sits opposite Cal, and they drink their tea in silence. He's had a haircut, she notices.

'You are a good friend,' Roisin says.

'Aye, a know,' he replies.

He reaches out and puts his hand over hers, and Roisin tries not to cry.

And then she goes through to her room and falls asleep on the sofa. She watches the anklet on the bed. It burns into her eyes as she drifts.

SIX: SEPTEMBER

NOW THAT THE HEATWAVE has broken it feels as though it never happened at all.

Roisin has been without a phone or keys for a week, but it feels like a relief. She gets up before Cal, because if she wants to leave the flat she has to do so in the evenings or the early mornings before he leaves for work so he can let her back in. She goes for walks to Leith Links, or Holyrood Park if she has the time.

During the day she spends her time cleaning or watching TV. Yesterday she cleaned the whole bathroom from top to bottom. She even washed the shower curtain. Cal is still watching too much telly, and so is she, but *Love Island* has thankfully ended so there is not quite the same frantic desperation to their shite binges now, which is nice.

Cal has said he will cover her rent this month. He did a huge Asda delivery the other day. He has been cooking her food. Yesterday Roisin cooked for them instead. It was horrible – she burnt the garlic – but he ate it anyway.

She planted the rhododendrons in the tenement's shared garden the other day too. It was fucking horrible: Roisin discovered more than one cat shit while she dug, but she couldn't sit and watch the plants continue to die, and throwing them out felt like murder.

Right now Roisin is sitting on the floor in her room alphabetising Cal's books because she has run out of things to do. It is just as she is reaching G that the buzzer goes. She assumes it's Cal, but when she peers out into the stairwell it is to find Claire on her way up the spiral steps carrying a Topping & Co tote bag.

'Hello,' Roisin says.

'Hi.'

Roisin remembers that she is supposed to be furious with her and thinks that she probably shouldn't let her in, but she doesn't really have the energy and so she lets her walk past her through the door and into the flat.

Claire sits down at the kitchen table. Roisin puts the kettle on.

Roisin has never seen her here before. It's funny how different people appear out of their usual environments. Claire doesn't look quite right here, framed against the whitewashed walls. She sits awkwardly with one leg folded underneath herself.

Roisin wonders how she knew where the kitchen was. She must have been here before. Roisin tries not to think too much about this.

'I brought your things,' she says, reaching into the tote bag. Roisin's clothes have been washed and neatly folded. They look unrecognisable. Roisin thinks Claire might have cleaned her phone case. Or paid someone else to clean her phone case. She's definitely cleaned Roisin's bag; it too was a victim in the seagull-shite incident.

'Thank you,' Roisin says.

Claire fiddles with a leather band around her wrist and asks how Roisin has been without looking at her face. Roisin shrugs and returns the question. Claire shrugs too.

The kettle clicks off, and Roisin goes to the window to make tea. It's a relief to do something with her hands.

'I've missed you,' Claire says to her back.

Roisin doesn't reply. She has not missed her.

Roisin decides to make tea in a teapot. She fishes out Cal's delicate flowered teacups and decants the milk into a matching jug. The whole effect is a wee bit more granny than she intended but it is better than the alternatives: the only other clean mugs are an ancient SNP *Bairns not bombs* one or the one that's shaped like a boob. Claire looks faintly impressed by the set-up, or maybe Roisin is projecting.

'Have you found another job then?' Claire asks, clearly deciding to pretend as though she didn't say anything else.

Roisin shakes her head. 'Not yet.'

'Oh well,' she says. 'You're young, you've got the rest of your life to figure it out.'

Roisin nods, even though she doesn't: she has until the end of the month because she can't ask Cal to cover her again.

'What sort of work are you looking for?' Claire asks.

'Pretty much anything at this point,' Roisin says.

Claire nods, and then asks her to come back to her.

'I miss you. And I think we were good together. I think you really understood me in a way nobody ever has.'

She reaches out and pours them both more tea even though Roisin hasn't finished her cup yet.

'It hasn't been the same without you. There was a housewarming last weekend, and I just know Eve misses you too. Everyone does. You know Oak is due in a couple of months. She was asking after you too. Well, she was asking Eve about you. Apparently you two haven't seen each other much recently.'

She is quite strange-looking really, Roisin thinks,

as she surveys her. It's as though her head is much too small for her body.

Roisin still hasn't sat down, she stands awkwardly by the sink, gripping tight to her teacup. Claire is looking at her. Roisin looks down.

It would be so easy to say yes. Things could go back to the haze of summer, and Roisin wouldn't have to work, or worry about bills or anything really. She could drink at parties at mad houses in Marchmont and Morningside and Stockbridge and watch TV on Claire's massive flat-screen and use her expensive shampoo, except now it would be Roisin's expensive shampoo. Or she could just sit on the bus all day, if she wanted to.

Claire finishes her tea in one long gulp and pours herself another. Then she looks around the kitchen.

'I like how you've decorated,' she says. But Roisin notices her eyes hang on the cobwebs in the corner of the ceiling and the spots of dark mould above the hob that are too high for Cal and her to reach.

This, for some reason, is what finally makes Roisin realise that she hates her.

After Claire has left, Roisin puts her clothes in the washing machine. She puts it on a really high heat – not caring if they shrink – and adds in twice the recommended amount of washing powder. She sits on the floor of the kitchen and watches it spin for a bit, and then she leans over to the fridge and nicks one of Cal's blueberry yoghurts, except it's not stealing because he did the shop for both of them, and Roisin has written it all down and she will pay him back.

She stands up and puts her phone on charge. It lights up with messages from Cal from the night it died, asking where she's been all night and when will she get back and let him know she's safe. And then emails from Holland and Barrett. Instagram notifications: two new bots tried to follow her. There is nothing from Eve. Roisin didn't expect there to be. Roisin wants some sort of reassurance that she is safe, but maybe it's better not knowing.

Roisin turns her phone back off and hides it under a pile of angry TV licence notice letters. And then she goes back to her room and lies on her bed and stares at the shapes on the ceiling.

*

Roisin wakes at seven o'clock in the morning. As though she is a Sim and the thirteen-year-old controlling her has pressed the *get dressed* button, she gets out of bed the moment she wakes. She pulls on one of Cal's jumpers and his jacket and puts the anklet in her pocket, and then she goes into the bathroom and splashes her face with some water, brushes her teeth, runs a comb through her hair, laces up her boots and leaves.

She has her keys back. She can leave whenever she wants. They jingle hopefully against the metal anklet in her pocket.

She starts off up Easter Road in the drizzle. Edinburgh suits the rain. She can't think of another city that suits the rain like Edinburgh does. The buildings lean in close to inhale the haar which has hitchhiked over from the Firth of Forth. You feel as though they are sheltering you more than normal buildings would. It feels like a relief, rain at last. Edinburgh has come back home.

Roisin can't remember who said Edinburgh was a city of shifting light, but it always seemed to her that it was a city of shifting dark instead. Edinburgh is always waiting for winter. It only starts to become its old self again when the pale night starts creeping in with the moon at 5 o'clock and the twisted trees bend with crab apples that overripen and squelch on the cracked pavement underfoot.

Or honestly maybe Edinburgh is just waiting for the fucking Fringe to finish. Even now Londoners throng the streets and flyers litter the pavement, and Roisin saw last week that the poor metal giraffes outside the Omni Centre have bright pink stickers advertising shows called stuff like *SLUT FEST! THE REUNION* plastered to their buttocks.

Roisin splashes along the road past Holyrood Palace and then down towards the loch under the old chapel ruins. Swans drift along, curled up like full stops, sleeping.

She doesn't stop to think about it, she walks firmly and with purpose. With one movement, she pulls the anklet out of her pocket and tosses it, underhand, into the thick, silty water.

There is a satisfying splash, then a perfect wee ripple, then another and another and another and then all trace of it is gone and Roisin can see the sky reflected back at her.

She turns, smiling, and squelches her way along the path which circles the loch and up the hill. Her heavy boots are already caked in mud. She pauses when she reaches the ruins, out of breath. Then she keeps going, up each rough stone ledge. The wind is biting, but she's grateful for it because she's already sweating through Cal's jumper.

As she reaches the top of Arthur's Seat she can see from the Pentland Hills at her back all the way over to Leith and down to the ribbon of light flowing between the Firth and the sea. It's like she's breathing properly for the first time in months. When she left the flat the streetlamps were still bright, but now the sun has overpowered them, and Edinburgh has come back to life.

SEPTEMBER

It feels to Roisin like she could be the only person in the world. Maybe this could be enough.

Then she laughs out loud, letting it echo along the rocks and down into the city. She tells herself to stop being such a wank and picks her way back down the hill, stopping for milk on the way home.

A NOTE ON THE AUTHOR

ALESSANDRA THOM is a writer from Aberdeenshire. She was a Scottish Book Trust New Writers Awardee for Prose in 2023 and the runner-up in the Short Fiction International Short Story Prize 2024. Her short fiction has appeared in *Gutter*. *Summer Hours* is her first novel.

ACKNOWLEDGEMENTS

THE FIRST DRAFT OF this book was written in a frenzy over a very hot summer in 2022. It is the result of a specific kind of madness, and of the support of the lovely people I had around me.

To Ben, Martha, James and Rory, first and foremost, always.

To my mum and dad, for everything I am.

To Matthew and Joseph, and all my extended family.

To Erin, Sally, Cat.

To Nicole Sellew, who read countless iterations of this book, and made it better each time.

To my agent Seren Adams, for taking me seriously as a writer and for thoughtful, inspired edits.

To Edward Crossan, Jennifer Andreacchi, Ellen Cranston, Kathryn Haldane, Sarah Ream, Abigail Salvesen and the whole team at Polygon for creativity, enthusiasm, meticulous attention to detail and for loving the book enough to take it on.

To the late John Burnside (who gleefully told me he hated Roisin), Daisy Lafarge, Dina Nayeri and to the entire Prose MLitt 21-22 cohort at St Andrews for your insight with early chapters of this and support beyond the degree programme.

To the Robert Nicol Trust, who provide financial support to students from the Aberdeen region.

To the Scottish Book Trust, particularly Eilidh Akilade and Lynsey Rogers, and the whole 2023 New Writers Award cohort.

To Oli, and the Peckham Pelican writer's group.

To the staff at the St Andrews SU bar, Starbucks on Leith Walk, BookBar, Forest Hill Library, the Honor Oak Pub, the Peckham Pelican and LNER trains.

And to the friends I don't talk to anymore. It's a strange love, that.